"Tabbie's original and unusual plots and storylines make for a really intriguing read."
Dave Andrews, Presenter, *BBC Radio Leicester*

"The master of supernatural suspense."
Peter J Bennett, *Author*

"The books are catching, they keep you thinking, and make you 'look outside the box'. I enjoy reading Tabbie's books in my limited down time."
Anne Royle and Spook (my four legged glasses).
Founder *Pathfinder Guide Dog Programme*

"Tabbie's skilful tale weaving grips, shocks and inspires every time and leaves you feeling that these narratives are coming with a deeper message from the world of Spirit. I always look forward to each new novel that she has crafted, with great anticipation."
Karen, *Indigo Aura Spiritual*

"Be prepared for the unexpected. Tabbie will exercise your memory, imagination and emotions as she guides you through a wonderful journey. Tabbie is a genuine kind, loving and wise soul. She will take you to another level of enlightenment."
Chris, *CV Holistic therapies*

For Marie
Best Wishes
Tabbie

When They Recall Your Spirit

Other Books by this Author

THE JENNY TRILOGY
White Noise is Heavenly Blue
The Spiral
Choler

A Fair Collection
The Unforgivable Error
No-Don't!
Above The Call
A Bit Of Fresh
A Bit Of Spare
The Paws Of Spiritual Justice
Sever His Member
The Hole Will Get You

NOTICE
Please note that the author's website
www.tabbiebrowneauthor.com
has now been closed.
For information on all books,
please visit Amazon where they are available
in paperback and also on Kindle.
Also check her Author Central page.
You can also buy paperbacks direct from Lulu Publishing.

When They Recall Your Spirit

Tabbie Browne

Copyright © 2020 Tabbie Browne

All rights reserved, including the right to reproduce this book, or portions thereof in any form. No part of this text may be reproduced, transmitted, downloaded, decompiled, reverse engineered, or stored, in any form or introduced into any information storage and retrieval system, in any form or by any means, whether electronic or mechanical without the express written permission of the author.

This is a work of fiction. Names and characters are the product of the author's imagination and any resemblance to actual persons, living or dead, is entirely coincidental.

The views expressed in this work are solely those of the author and do not necessarily reflect the views of the publisher, and the publisher hereby disclaims any responsibility for them.

ISBN: 9798653481246

PublishNation
www.publishnation.co.uk

This book is dedicated to:

Pat

My sister-in-law who had every one of my books. Born in England, but moved to Canada and then lived in many states in the USA. She loved Arizona because she said it was so spiritual and that is where she passed away June 2020.

Chapter 1

Russ looked at his watch again. He almost wallowed in the time he was alone for that was when he was at peace. His mother was a God fearing woman who had brought him up to go to all the church services and Sunday school and was still peeved that he had given up going with her when he was in his early twenties. There had been many rows followed by days of silence as she let her disappointment hit home. Her husband had died when Russ was young and she was determined to have her only child brought up as a Christian and hopefully enter the church when he felt the call. But that never came.

He was in the kitchen checking the vegetables on the stove when she came through the front door and immediately his body tensed. What would be wrong today?

"Well," Irene began before he had chance to greet her "Mrs next door was showing of her new hat for all to see. Likes to swank she does. Don't overboil those potatoes. Have you put the roasts in?"

"Was she? I haven't. And yes." He knew she'd be annoyed. She always was when he answered all her comments together.

The answer was a 'Hmm." as she turned to go and take off her coat, hat and gloves.

"They always ask why you don't come any more." Irene had way of saying it as though it was the first time, yet you could almost predict the exact moment and where she would be standing as she announced it.

"And I expect you gave them the same reason as you always do Mother."

The tone was curt but Russ had learned to let the words float off his tongue with humour, thus preventing his stomach churning with frustration and anger. To be honest he was quite enjoying it because he knew she no longer had the upper hand.

"If only you knew, you silly old cow." He thought, which was his polite Sunday version of what normally exploded inside.

He was careful not to smirk at such times and usually turned his back just in case her eagle eyes should pick up a trace of his sarcasm.

The next act was predictable. Having donned her apron, Irene then proceeded to check every item from the oven to the top of the stove, the temperature of the plates and testing the gravy giving her usual running commentary as she did so. It hardly needs to be said that she found fault with everything. The only way Russ coped with this was to add his own silent asides.

"The sprouts aren't as hard as I like them."
"I'm surprised you liked anything hard."
"Have you laid the table?"
"That's not all I've laid."
"You never say much."
"No need. You say enough for the whole street."
"I'd have expected you to be married by now."
"But you wouldn't have approved of anyone I brought home."
"Did you turn the meat?"
"What I do with my meat is my business."

Until they were about to sit down for dinner she barely took a breath. He learned who had been to church, what they wore and any gossip that she could pick up. As they were eating he asked "So what does this church of yours teach you?"

The look cut the air.

"You shouldn't need to ask that. You used to go. You know what they teach you."

"You'll wear that word out." He smirked.

She stood back, hands on hips and faced him.

"Now you just listen to me my lad, you can knock that haughty expression off your face and start showing a bit of respect. You weren't brought up like that and I'm sure I don't know where or why you got such ideas. Acting above your station. Who do you think you are?"

He took a deep breath and said very calmly "Are we going to eat the dinner or let it go to waste?"

Each word was almost an arrow of hate as it left his mouth. Irene although taken aback, wasn't going to release her hold of this or any other similar situation.

"I think you had better wash your hands and sit down."

As he slowly made his way to the sink his eyes never left her which he knew made her feel very uncomfortable. He had been studying her closely and knew everything that unsettled her. To add to the insult, he slowly carried the plates and dishes into the dining area with absolute precision, making sure everything was perfectly placed. Her mouth opened as if to speak but on catching a glimpse of his face she closed it again, quickly.

She knew he was playing a little game and didn't know quite how to handle it. When he was little she could box his ears but now he was a man it was different. It was obvious he had no respect for her although to the outside world he was a dutiful son, looked after his mum, worked hard, and seemed pleasant enough but nobody knew the real him. He didn't socialise in the small town where they lived and when he went out in his car, nobody knew where, even Irene.

"I thought I'd ask your Auntie Vi to come for tea next Sunday. Make a nice change for her. She doesn't get out much now."

As she spoke she knew this wouldn't go down well, but it was one way of letting him know who was still boss in this house.

"You talk about her as though she was some poor old soul." He looked straight at her. "She's younger than you and she certainly doesn't sit around moping."

Irene sniffed.

"She puts a brave face on it but its not easy on your own, I should know."

He sighed quite loudly thinking "Here we go again." But what was the point of repeating himself. His mother was one to bemoan her fate whereas Aunt Vi was just the opposite. Although retired she helped local charities and still sang in a local ladies choir.

"We don't see enough of her and families should stick together." Irene wasn't going to let it drop.

Russ put his knife and fork down heavier than he intended and almost told his mother that the reason his aunt didn't come very much was because she couldn't stand her. She was her sister in law, having been married to Irene's brother so there was no blood tie.

Instead he said very slowly and precisely "I'm sure she comes whenever she wants, invitation or no invitation." As he let it sink in, he stood up and cleared the plates from the table. You could have cut the air with a knife. Irene got up, her mouth pursed showing she was peeved and got the pudding. The rest of the meal was in total silence which wasn't unusual but Russ knew he was getting to her. The problem was it wasn't having a good effect on his mental state and before long there would be danger of him blowing completely.

Violet Trewicke, although every bit as religious as her sister in law worshipped at another church and had very different views to those held by Irene which was frowned upon at any opportunity. Russ always felt that his mother did it mainly for show to prove what a good person she was, but apart from going to services and the occasional fund raising event, she spent most of her time talking about it but doing very little. Some of the congregation were giving her a wide berth as they were never sure of where their comments would be shared.

Vi on the other hand was the first one to roll up her sleeves and get on with anything that needed doing. If anyone was ill or going through a bad time, she would do what she could to see them through whether it be shopping or running errands, fetching prescriptions etc. Yet she never bragged about it or disclosed any information she was privy to learn. Whether it was jealousy, which is often the root of most things, or not, Irene would often describe her as belonging to one of those other so called religions.

Russ had always liked her and admired the way she wouldn't let his mother rule her. He knew that if there was an invitation to tea, there would be an ulterior motive such as finding out the latest gossip.

"Should be fun." He thought as he remembered Irene's passing suggestion. It meant that something was going on and she couldn't wait until she knew what it was and as her church people weren't forthcoming, Vi was the obvious target.

Market Riverbrook where they all lived was a reasonably sized town only a few miles from the nearest city so was quite a busy place. It had grown over recent years when new houses had been added along with inevitable supermarkets but the attractive outdoor and indoor market still thrived with locally grown country produce. The name dated back many years. All the local villages had a picturesque little stream, or brook running alongside the main streets and where these converged the town grew. It attracted many visitors much to the delight of local traders.

Fortunately, it was large enough for anyone to be private if they wished. There were many little 'pockets', almost like self contained villages where everybody could know everyone else's business if they wanted to. Obviously Irene Marsh lived in such an area. She wouldn't have had it otherwise. Vi on the other hand preferred to keep her own affairs to herself. She was the first one to help anyone in need, but anything she heard was never repeated. This was what made Irene so annoyed. You could never find out anything important, well important to her that is.

It was late afternoon when the phone rang. Vi was half asleep and reached for the handset.

"Hello." She sounded drowsy.

"It's me, I thought you might like to come for tea next week."

Irene was obviously waiting for a reply without further details.

Vi looked at the phone. "No greeting, no how are you. Just a summons." She thought. She took a deep breath.

"Presuming you mean next Sunday, I'm afraid I can't but thanks anyway."

To her that was enough. She didn't have to give any explanation.

"Oh. That's a pity. We haven't had a chat for weeks and we don't want to get out of touch do we?"

"She wants information or just being nosey." Vi smirked but said "Oh I'm sure we won't do that. Some other time. Must go. Bye."

She ended the call knowing Irene would be furious as she would be sniffing for gossip as usual. Why else would she ring? Before she had time to think, the phone went again but she could see by the number it was a friend of hers and after a few moments she had almost forgotten her sister in law.

Irene of course was livid. How dare anyone cut her off like that without even a 'by your leave' as she put it. That could only mean one thing. Vi must have something she didn't want to talk about so that made her even more curious and she was determined to find out. Russ walked through to the kitchen to get a drink.

"Well, there's a thing! Your aunt was very curt with me so there's something she's not saying."

Russ sighed loudly.

"Only you could think a thing like that Mother."

"But she chopped me off before I had chance to say anything."

He stopped and faced her.

"Has it ever occurred to you that she doesn't want to talk to you. Or she may have been watching a film. Or having a little sleep. Or…she had somebody there."

He knew he had lit the touch paper.

"Somebody there. A man you mean? Well, I….she couldn't… I mean…."

"I'm not saying she had. But she doesn't have to fill in a log book for you every time she moves."

Her face was a picture. She sat there mouth open, her mind going through every possibility. He knew it was wrong but he got a sadistic pleasure playing with her thoughts and emotions. Leaving her to stew, he slowly went out of the room with a malicious grin of self satisfaction.

In the safety of his own space he settled down for a conversation, and although there appeared to be no one there, the air was electric with one who was always part of him.

When one thinks of twins it is usually on a physical level. Whether identical or not they will have been born to one earth mother but how often do people say of someone close to them "we are so alike we could have been twins."

The answer is because they are. On the spiritual level one soul can occupy two bodies and they don't have to have entered the world at the same time. Also two spirits can be born simultaneously and live their earth lives in close proximity. It all depends upon the tasks they are placed to perform. It is so easy to forget that we are all here for a reason but some are very aware of the purpose and will go to any lengths to fulfil it.

In this case Russ's twin, Denzil was solely in spirit. He was not a guardian as they both had their own angels but they always operated as twins, physically as male, female or one of each depending on the task of the moment. But this was a very different case. It was necessary for one to be in placement on earth and the other free to observe with the freedom of total spirit. They were well aware it could be highly dangerous and threaten their existence in any form. Although until recently, neither had been in bodily existence for sometime, the highly trained evil watchers could pick them out in an instant so they had to be on full alert constantly, but without it being obvious. This is a hard task in itself for the slightest slip could ruin the whole objective and watchers are everywhere, usually in the most unexpected places. Even an odd glance could break a cover. There was also the problem that with only one being in earth form, that could in itself raise awareness so plans were in place to draw the attention away if necessary.

Their communication lasted less than a millisecond and their guardians were hovering to create a false image of their meeting. This was done by changing air patterns. If you are talking to someone you care for, the surrounding space has a very different colour and feel to one where enemies are in conflict. That is an extreme, but there are myriads of levels in between and observers are very quick to pick up on any change or anything that doesn't fit with the situation.

Russ now knew his next move although he let nothing about his aura portray it. High spirits can mask excitement, anger, love or any emotion and reaction to news, so although he had been updated, no entity could have guessed what his intention would be.

Denzil himself had gone as quickly as he came and by instinct the two guardians did not communicate any of the interchange.

They were in normal contact because if they weren't, that itself would have drawn attention to them, for twins are always close. Also, Denzil had left a decoy, a highly experienced spirit that could assume any form and this was the one who was now sharing Russ's room. It would stay for a reasonable time then calmly wander off which was the usual way so that everything appeared completely normal.

Irene looked at her watch. It was getting on for tea time and she mustn't be late for evensong. Her fingers tapped the arm of her chair. She knew there would now be another exchange regarding the meal. Either that son of hers wouldn't want to come down, or he would and she'd have to put up with those horrible little snide remarks of his.

"Oh, I'll get it ready and he will have to please himself." She huffed as she got up and went into the kitchen. She jumped as he appeared behind her.

"You startled me, creeping up on people like that. I could have had a heart attack."

He smiled. "Should I go out and come in again?"

"Oh, to see if it works you mean. I don't know where you get your callous humour from, I really don't. Your dad would have been shocked at you."

Russ stood very solemnly, his hands together and his head bowed in mock reverence.

"Forgive me for I have sinned."

He could hardly stop laughing especially when his mother went into one of her rants. After a moment he held up his hand and said quietly "Shall I put the kettle on?"

She spluttered lost for words at his impudence and waved him aside saying "If you can manage it."

He knew he had won and so did she but she didn't know how to handle it. For years she had lost control over his behaviour and there was no way of changing him now. But for how much longer could she stand it? She felt as though she was loosing her mind.

"There we are Mother dear. Tea is brewing. What would you like me to do now?"

"Um, I. ..oh just take the crockery in."

This threw her. If he was being nice there had to be a reason for it. She put the food on the table and checked she had got everything. He timed it to when she was taking her first bite.

"You know Mother, you are always begging me to come to church with you...."

She cut in "Let's not go into all that again, I want to have my tea in peace."

He smiled. "Well, I though I might come with you this evening."

Apart from her spluttering, there was silence for a moment. Then she looked at him.

"If this is one of your silly games to get me annoyed......."

"No game Mother. I'll come if you would like me to. That's all there is to it."

The air was still.

"You know I would like it. Haven't I said so often enough?"

"That's settled then."

Her expression was priceless. A mixture of relief but also disbelief tinged with a little caution.

"Right. Good. We must leave here at six."

She still was not sure of what was going on but wasn't going to refuse him. As he made his way to his room to get ready, the satisfied smirk appeared.

"Well I think that went ok."

No onlooker would have been aware of the silent acknowledgment he received.

The atmosphere in Violet's home was altogether different. She hummed as she got ready for church, making sure she had everything she needed, for there was going to be a little meeting after the service to discuss the arrangements for the summer fair which was imminent. Originally it was to be an outdoor event but as the weather didn't seem to realise it should be warm, everyone suggested they move it to the church hall to be on the safe side. Violet was going to run a craft stall as she was very creative and had made some very attractive items. The helpers didn't call themselves a committee as they liked to keep everything as informal as possible and no one tried to outshine anyone else. This was one way they differed from Irene's church where there was always one who knew better than everybody and expected things to be done her way.

Having changed and done her hair, Violet was ready to go. She had a small car but as the church was so near she always walked. When she was about half way there, she felt as though she wasn't alone and instinctively turned round to see who was following her, but there was nobody close. A few other people were about but this was something different. She carried on and was glad the evenings were light for she would have been very uneasy had it been dark. She almost ran the last few steps and as she got to the small entrance foyer she had to catch her breath. Janet, who was just coming out of the toilet passed her and then stopped.

"What's the matter Vi, you look a bit flustered." And she took her by the arm to a nearby seat.

"I..I'm alright, thank you." Her pulse was still racing.

"Well, you sit quiet for a minute." She had enough sense not to pester her friend but knew something had unnerved her. She sat on the seat near her and said "Take your time."

After a few moments, Vi shook herself and said "Oh thank you for not fussing Janet. I just, I mean, well it will sound silly."

"Nothing is silly if it's upset you. I could tell you some tales."

After a moment Vi explained the sensation she had felt and before she could suggest it was her imagination, Janet cut in.

"I've had it. Where did you feel it, I mean exactly where were you?"

Vi felt a flood of relief flow over her.

"Well I was just passing that house with the trees in front, you can hardly see the house and then...."

"Just when you turned the corner you felt it." Janet finished it off for her.

"Well yes, that's right, but you've never said."

"I know. Didn't want people to think I'd lost my marbles."

They were both quiet for a moment then Vi said "We aren't going crazy are we? I mean, not if we've both felt it."

Janet looked at her for a minute then whispered "I'm not supposed to say this but we aren't the only ones."

"What!"

"Ssshh. We'll talk later, away from here."

They were interrupted by the door to the church opening and a lady popped her head round.

"Oh there you are. Come on. I thought it was funny if you two were late. We can start now." She gave them both a searching look.

Janet was quick to pick up on this and said "Oh Vi was a bit out of puff, told her she shouldn't have hurried."

Even if no words were uttered, the atmosphere was loaded, as if everyone knew exactly what had happened.

Denzil was back in situ and as Russ sat in church with his mother, the two males exchanged knowing images. Irene was almost showing off the fact that her son did come to church hoping it would be one in the eye for the scandal mongers. This would be all round the local area by tonight, well it would save her doing the job.

To the outsider, Russ appeared to be a very happy carefree young man with a permanent little smile on his face. If they only knew what lay behind it, for it was no benevolent smile, it was a sadistic smirk. Although his body may have been in a place of worship, his spirit was hard at work and before long people would be feeling the outcome. This was the perfect building to get all the so called little do gooders in one place instead of having to go out and find them all. For these were the self righteous holier than thou, look down on everyone else brigade and they would be easy prey. They hid under the umbrella of 'because we go to church we are good and you are not'. He'd even heard his mother say it. Well, things were about to rock their little boat and he couldn't wait.

His thoughts were interrupted by Denzil.

"We've had our knuckles rapped."

"Oh, they want results. Yes I got the message."

"No. You didn't."

While this exchange was going on, Russ appeared to be singing the hymn which was all for show. But he was curious at his partner's reply.

"What do you mean, I didn't."

"Because they called me on my own. You are too intent on your own vendetta, but we are here to do a job and they want it done."

"Well you have to include your own bit of amusement on the side."

If Denzil could have sighed he would. Although he also enjoyed the sidelines, as he called them, his objective was to get this job over and then be ready for the next. Russ had always been the laid back one, and could be extremely efficient if only he put his whole being into it but getting his sadistic amusement always had to come into it. Denzil liked him but he could be so exasperating. However, there was always the fact that Russ's apparent indolent attitude could mask his particular talent. During a task, his mind could appear to be oblivious to what was going on around him, but his spirit never missed a thing. On many occasions he came up with every factor needed to finish a job, every bit of evidence supported, and yet had appeared to be uninterested from start to finish.

Denzil's reply was curt.

"Well as soon as you've finished playing with these innocent little souls, could you spare a minute to concentrate on our instructions please?" He emphasised that last word.

There was a short pause before the reply came.

"Ahead of you old man."

Chapter 2

The little church to which Violet belonged was a fairly new building as opposed to the old stone built one that Irene attended. The church hall was attached and used for many different functions. Whereas old buildings are often supposed to be a bit spooky with tales of ghostly happenings, this didn't have anything like that. The general atmosphere was friendly and everyone was greeted and made to feel welcome.

When Vi had arrived feeling very shaken, the calmness of the place soon made her feel better and she felt safe. But then she knew she had to go home and her apprehension grew as the evening wore on. Janet was sitting next to her and passed the occasional smile of reassurance and as the service finished she whispered "Don't worry, I'll come with you."

"Oh you don't have to do that but….."

"But you'd feel better if I did." Janet finished it for her.

"Well if I'm honest, but I feel so silly."

As they put on their coats after the meeting and said good night to the rest of the helpers, the vicar took her hand and held it for a moment. She felt she had to look him in the face.

"You are never alone." He whispered in a loving tone and with a gentle nod of his head he directed her to Janet.

When they were out of earshot she said "I wonder why he said that."

Janet just smiled but Vi was looking for answers.

"I feel there's something you aren't telling me."

Janet bypassed it by saying "Fancy coming back to mine for a cuppa?"

"Um, that's very kind but I think I need to get home, if you don't mind."

"Tell you what then," Janet wasn't giving up as though there was something she had to tell her friend "go home, make a drink and I will give you a ring."

"Well alright."

They had reached the spot by the house where Vi had felt strange. Instinctively she slowed her pace but Janet said "Keep walking and look ahead."

It came out as an order and Vi wasn't going to argue for the quicker she was past the place the better.

"Will you be alright from here?"

Vi jumped.

"Oh sorry, yes thank you, I will be fine."

Janet walked a few more paces then turned off towards her own house.

"Don't forget I'll be ringing."

She called over her shoulder without turning but Vi had a strong feeling that her friend was hurrying away from here for some reason.

When Irene and Russ got home, he went to go to his room but she stopped him and said "Well? Did you like it?"

"It wasn't so bad." There was no smile, no warmth, not even a snide remark from him.

She wasn't leaving it there.

"So you'll come again, do you think?"

He was halfway up the stairs by now.

"Most likely." Was all she got as his door closed.

She hung up her coat and sat in the armchair for a moment. It would seem normal for her to have felt achievement, after all she had been going on at him long enough to go to church again, and then when he did, it had left a strange feeling inside. Questions started running through her head. He must have had a reason, but why? It certainly wasn't to please her. Was there someone, a young lady perhaps that he wanted to see? But he hadn't shown any interest in anyone there and she suspected that he couldn't have named even one of them.

A cup of tea was called for and she automatically went to the stairs to call up and ask if he wanted one but something stopped her and she went to the kitchen and made one for herself. That in itself was strange. Although she didn't realise it, she was no longer in control.

Russ lay flat on his back. His guardian knew this was a time to be watchful although his charge was adept at protecting himself in any circumstances. Watchers are always lurking for 'weak times'. This is when a person in body or totally in spirit communicates with those on a higher level or transmits highly confidential information which can be infiltrated. The spirits have their own ways of blocking, cloaking and scrambling messages. The good forces try to be one step ahead, but there are equally skilful evil powers waiting to intercept. It is not unlike modern physical communication methods but on a much higher scale.

The likes of Denzil and Russ had their own codes. Friends often have secret words to describe people they see without appearing disrespectful but this pair had an entire vocabulary, and it was constantly changing. It must be remembered that they didn't have to arrange such things, it was done in an instant. Probably hard to imagine if one isn't on that level, in fact it is a totally different way of existence to what most of us are aware.

In the blink of an eye, the pair had exchanged as much as it would take someone in body to say in about 2 hours. The guardians instinctively knew when to resume their normal protection although they were unaware of any exchanges.

Russ appeared in the lounge. Irene looked up surprised but glad he had come down.

"Like a cup of tea now?" She asked rather tentatively.

"Do you know, that would be nice. And if you've got one of those little cakes going spare......"

"Oh I have, I think I'll have one as well."

She was still in a slightly bewildered state so Russ thought he'd bring her back to normal.

"You not put any poison in this time have you?"

"Oh I thought there'd have to be something like that."

It seemed to bring her fight back and she sniffed loudly to show displeasure so he couldn't resist following on. As she handed him the plate with his cake on he peered at it and asked if he could examine hers as well. That did it.

"Well I did hope that you going to church would do you some good, but it's not made a scrap of difference has it?"

"So you don't want me to come again? Oh what a pity, just when I was beginning to enjoy myself too." The snide tone hung in the air.

She looked at him for a moment then, not wanting to appear that he'd got his own way said "Oh please yourself. I've given up trying to turn you into a decent person. You do what you want. You always have."

He sipped his tea, put his cup on the side table and said very slowly and precisely "I can do as I please. Hmm. Well I think I will go again then."

Her expression was priceless. She was speechless and just stared at him. The strange thing was that she had got her own way by getting him to go, but now he had agreed she had a weird uneasy feeling. Something didn't feel right and she felt the urge to tell him he couldn't, but somehow the words stuck in her throat. Her mind was going round and round.

"Perhaps he's just showing off and he'll have forgotten all about it by next week." She thought, but inwardly knew that wouldn't be the case.

Denzil had witnessed this little playacting and began to wonder just how much this was part of Russ's tactic. But what had it to do with their current assignment? Unless of course his partner wasn't divulging everything even to him.

The phone ringing startled Vi even though she was expecting the call. Although she guessed it was Janet calling as planned, she felt a bit apprehensive as she was still a bit shaky.

"Hello?"

Silence. There was obviously somebody on the end of the line but they weren't speaking.

She repeated. "Hello, who is this?"

Again no reply so she hit the button and almost tossed the handset down. It rang again immediately and she jumped before slowly picking it up. This time she didn't speak.

"Is that you Vi?" Janet's familiar voice was a relief.

"Yes, it is. Did you ring just now?"

"I did but you didn't answer. I was asking if you were there but you didn't say anything. Oh, I wonder if I dialled the wrong number."

Violet took a breath.

"I had a call but there was nobody there, at least they didn't speak."

"Oh no!" Janet sounded worried.

"What is it?"

"Well this happened some time back and we thought there was a prankster mucking about and upsetting people on their own. The phone would go and nobody was there, or at least they didn't speak."

"And you think they are doing it again. Well it's a pity they haven't got anything better to do than go around annoying people." Vi felt a bit relieved that maybe she wasn't being targeted on her own.

"Well it's not quite that simple." Janet's voice trailed off.

Now Vi didn't feel so calm.

"In what way?"

Janet paused as she knew that what she was going to say would take some believing.

"Are you sitting down?" she began.

"Yes. I am now." Vi was trembling but tried to keep her voice still.

"Well, it got so bad that the phone people tapped the line so they could trace the callers."

"And?"

"There were none."

Vi thought for a moment.

"So nobody rang while they tapped the lines."

Janet took a deep breath knowing what she was about to say would sound crazy.

"No calls were made to the numbers – at the time the phones rang."

Now both were quiet.

"Now let me get this right." Vi was trying to make sense of it. "The phones rang, somebody picked them up, there was no dialling tone so somebody was ringing but nobody answered and the telephone people had no trace of anyone making the call."

"You've got it exactly. And it went on for about a week or so then just stopped."
Vi wanted to find a simple answer.
"Well what if…..No can't be that…. I know…." But there was no answer.
Janet let it sink in before she added "There is something else."
Vi felt a cold shiver run down her back and she wasn't entirely sure if she wanted to know any more, but curiosity got the better of her.
"You'd better tell me then."
Janet paused but knew she had to say it.
"You felt funny when you passed that house tonight."
"Well yes but…….oh no you can't be saying that had anything to do with it."
"Only some people get that horrible feeling, and they are the ones that got the weird phone calls. Now you've had one."
Vi was shaking but still clinging onto a physical source.
"So someone is playing tricks aren't they."
"Oh yes? So how do they make some of us feel threatened near that house?"
Vi's brain was racing.
"Is it people on their own? Just women for instance?"
"No. Couples. Young folk, widows like us, and widowers, not just women, and they all feel it. Some won't go by, they either walk on the other side of the road or get dropped off. And don't forget it goes round the bend as well. It's all that corner."
"But it seems to come from the house because that's where I felt it first and it was almost following me."
"I know. You don't have to explain. I'm just sorry you are one of the….well ….people."
Vi sighed.
"I'm going to have to take all this in. Are you sure we aren't imagining it? Well no we can't be because I felt it. Oh I don't know."
"Look, at least you've got people to talk to who are in the same boat." Janet tried to reassure her but was trying to cope with it herself.

This whole situation was what Denzil and Russ had been discussing and they knew they had a mammoth task ahead of them. It wasn't the first time such a thing had happened but it was on the increase. Whereas it used to be the odd isolated case near an old empty house, it had now become something that could spring up anywhere, even on a new housing estate. But a pattern seemed to be forming recently. The buildings concerned had been occupied but as soon as they became empty something sinister began to happen almost as though something unseen had moved in and taken possession.

A typical example had happened recently in a neighbouring town. Right in the centre a small shop had become empty and was about to be used by a charity. But nobody could go in. When any helpers had tried to enter to give the place a coat of paint to brighten it up, they couldn't open the door. Thinking they had been given the wrong keys it was found that they were the set the previous occupier had left so had to be right. A locksmith was brought in to change the locks but as soon as he started work he had the strongest feeling of evil encompassing him and he had to leave. It happened to whoever tried to enter so in the end they called in a vicar to cleanse the place. He didn't even get near the front door when he was thrown back and landed on the ground. He was extremely shocked and all he could say to those who were helping him up was "Get away from this place, all of you." Then he passed out.

The strange thing was that the shops on either side were alright but the feeling of pure evil emanating from the empty one was affecting trade as nobody wanted to walk anywhere near it. Then as quickly as it started, it finished. It could have taken ages for anyone to find out but as luck would have it a few rowdy young men, a bit the worse for wear, or to put it bluntly blind drunk, were wandering down the path where the shop was. They decided it would be fun to smash a few windows so they hurled anything they could lay their hands on at the place. One even ventured in through the hole in the door but there was no fun in that so he came, or rather fell back out. This seemed highly amusing especially as one of his mates was taking the opportunity to have a pee in that particular spot just as he emerged so he got a face full.

When the local police arrived they dealt with them accordingly but one officer who was familiar with this area queried how they had even dared to go in or in fact even manage it when nobody else could. It may have been that they were pissed, as he put it, but his 'nose' told him it didn't add up. Apart from getting the shop secured he got a vicar he knew to give it the once over as soon as it was daylight.

It wasn't something anyone would have wanted to do but this clergyman trusted his policeman friend as they had known each other for years and if he said it was ok, then it was ok. Together with other volunteers they approached the shop. It was noticeable that they didn't slow their steps but walked straight up to the door. The vicar turned to his friend and said "It is clear, there is nothing evil here." With that he blessed the place and everyone left.

"You didn't seem the least bit wary." The officer said as they walked to his car.

"No. It was completely clear of anything untoward. I knew that before we were even near."

"I won't ask."

"Probably best."

Janet knew all about the incident but decided not to mention it, for if Vi hadn't heard about it there was no need to add to her worries. And perhaps the same thing would happen with the house near them. She could but hope, and then everything would be alright and Vi would put it down to her imagination.

Russ was sitting with Irene watching the television, but he was in communication with Denzil. They knew the house in question was more than just a red herring which the shop had been. Evil spirits were very adept at leading false trails to get the attention away from what was really going on. By raising strange but similar happenings around the area, people soon reacted with "Oh not again" or "It's only another one." Which was just what they intended. Meanwhile they could plant their seeds unnoticed ready for the big one.

Denzil and Russ knew that the house near Vi was not a distraction but the real thing. The fact that its power wasn't confined to the building and grounds but extended to the pavement and street all round the corner where it was situated worried them. They had to keep a close watch on the growth, that is the speed at which it was growing and also exactly where, but the reason was still unknown.

At times like this it was often necessary to have watchers posted from a distance and change them frequently so the evil didn't suspect they were under scrutiny, but it has to be remembered, these evil forces are not amateurs but highly toned masters in their field.

It had been recorded that since Vi first felt uneasy on the way to church, the evil had already spread backwards and was entering all the gardens at its rear. The reason for this was unclear but Russ was determined to have a closer look as soon as he was alone.

Vi was thinking about going to bed when her front door bell rang. She looked through the eyepiece and was surprised to see the vicar standing there. Quickly she opened the door.

"Hello vicar, come in."

He hesitated for a moment then slowly walked in. She thought he had a strange look about him and took him into the lounge where he sat down.

"You look concerned vicar." The words came out before she had time to stop them. Then she realised he wasn't looking at her but at the carpet.

"Um, this isn't easy for me to say Mrs Trewicke.....um.. Well I just want you to know that if you need someone to talk to, I'm always here for you."

Vi knew this wasn't what he had come for and was beginning to feel a bit uneasy.

He continued "There have been some rather unusual situations in the area of late and of course people always have their own ideas but they aren't always right."

Vi was watching him wishing he'd spit it out and get on with it. Not knowing quite how to react she said "Anything in particular vicar?"

"Well, there are always rumours of course, you get those anywhere but sometimes things aren't always of our understanding."

In the end her exasperation got the better of her.

"Vicar, I may be a bit thick here, but just what are you trying to tell me?"

He looked at her now.

"People often offer help in times of trouble you see but they aren't always the ones who can help, in fact just the opposite. They could be leading you up the wrong path."

With that he got up and hurried to the door and without turning said "Be careful who you trust, they are not always your friends."

He didn't even wait for her to open the door but grabbed it and rushed out leaving her - to put it bluntly - gob smacked.

"Well, what was all that about?" She sank into her chair and tried to remember what he had said, which wasn't very much. Then her mind wandered to what Janet had told her. After a moment she sat bolt upright as the possibility of the vicar's visit hit her. He was warning her, but he couldn't have known about her conversation with Janet. Then she remembered how he held her hand as they left the church and told her she wasn't alone and had looked towards her friend as he said it. She took that to mean she could trust her. But suddenly doubt came into her mind. His visit had been for a purpose, warning her to be careful who she trusted. Suddenly a strength seemed to fill her as though she was being protected which was true, as her guardian had put a protective cloak around her, knowing it would be necessary.

Russ and Denzil were now on high alert. They hadn't expected the vicar to make that move as it was exposing him to danger but there was an added problem. Sometimes the evil would infiltrate a holy person to hide until they were ready to strike. Was he aware of this and fighting while he could to warn Vi in case they took over? Immediately added protection was sent to help him and rid him of any strong evil force.

It was becoming clear to the high angels that the force surrounding the house on the corner was different to anything they had encountered in the past. Several sweeps had been done and something was there but not identifiable. Physically the house had been empty for sometime, the garden overgrown and it was rather sad that such a lovely place should be so desolate. But was this what they wanted? Hidden from passers by anything could go on there and of course if anyone did trespass there would be nothing to see. But on the spiritual level there was plenty of activity going on but by whom? This was the question to which Russ and Denzil had to find the answer. Their hierarchy didn't want too many investigators swamping the area or that could scare off whatever was there, but they had to know and soon. It was necessary to employ unusual tactics and if anyone could pull it off, this pair were the obvious choice. Their communication would be extra coded from now on and although they may appear to be enjoying silly banter, each syllable would be loaded with information and only passed to higher levels by secret means. They were very definitely now on the front line and exposed to the greatest danger possible.

Chapter 3

It was still cooler than usual for summer and Irene was wondering what to put on. Russ had gone to work and the feeling in the house was much lighter when he wasn't there, although she felt it wasn't very Christian like to admit it. He did seem to put a dampener on things and went out of his way to annoy her but apart from chastising him she had no idea as to the best way of controlling him. One minute she would feel she was winning and the next he would deflate her with that superior attitude of his.

But what she was lacking was a good old gossip. She had hoped Violet would have come but the woman wasn't very forthcoming and seemed to have different views which she didn't mind imparting. No, the answer had to be nearer home and about people she knew. Some of them at church would let a snippet drop now and again but actual tittle tattle was frowned upon. After a minute's consideration she had the answer.

"I'll go and see Lily." She said aloud.

This lady was in her early eighties and recently had become almost house bound which was sad as she had always been very active and the first to give help if it was needed. Her joints were witness to the amount of abuse they had received and now were very painful and restricted her movements. She had several neighbours who popped in and did bits of housework or shopping for her and she was always extremely grateful and never took anyone for granted.

Irene would go round today to give her some company, but it was unlikely she would do anything else except talk the poor woman to death! If she didn't get enough news she would leave with some excuse about having to visit someone else. But her hopes were on Lily as she got her things together. Most visitors would have taken something but Irene wasn't there to give, just receive.

The carer had just helped Lily to have her morning wash and was filling in her notes when the doorbell went.

"Oh, someone's at the door, I'll go." She offered as she put her books down.

Lily was thinking of who could be there and inwardly hoped it wasn't 'that nosey woman.'

"You've got a visitor Lily." The carer announced as she led Irene into the lounge.

"Oh, that's nice." The enthusiasm wasn't in her voice.

"Well I thought I'd just pop in and see how you are." Irene raised her voice.

The carer with her back to her looked at Lily with a wry smile for she knew what the poor soul was in for.

"I'm not deaf." Lily announced thinking "Why does she have to treat me like an old dear?"

The carer picked up her things and said "See you tomorrow Lily." Then turning to Irene said "I wouldn't tire her if I were you, she's not had a very good night."

After the front door had closed, Irene pulled up a chair so she was facing her.

"So, how have you been dear?"

"Fine thank you. And yourself?"

"I don't suppose you've been out much have you?"

"Not much."

By now Lily was hoping it wasn't going to be a long session because she knew exactly why this woman had come, but unless she could come up with a darned good reason, it could go on and on. Knowing the purpose of the visit was to dig for gossip, she wasn't about to feed her any news about anyone. There would be no proper conversation, for this annoying woman asked questions but never listened to the answers, and when she had fired about ten of them, she would start at number one again.

"So, who's been to see you?"

"Oh family you know. They're very good."

That went down like a fart in church so Irene had to come in from another angle.

"Any of your friends?"

25

"Don't think so."

"Oh, right, well I expect they are too busy, but they will."

There was silence for a moment so she had to try again.

"It was just the usual lot at church. But it's dwindling you know."

"I expect it is."

This was going nowhere, just as Lily wanted.

"So, nobody has been in with, well any news really."

Although it was supposed to sound casual it was so blatantly obvious what was being asked.

"No."

Lily was playing it to perfection and getting a sadistic pleasure out of dangling this nosey parker on her bit of string. Now it was time for the kill.

"It was nice of you to call Irene, but if you've come hoping to learn what anyone is doing, talking about or sleeping with, I'm afraid you've wasted your time."

"Well!" Irene stood up, her face red. "To think you have that opinion of me. I'm shocked."

Lily waited until she got to the door then played her trump card.

"It's only my legs don't work Irene, my brain is as sharp as ever. Good bye."

Russ was amused with the interchange and knew his mother would now be off elsewhere for her information as she needed the tittle tattle to keep her going, always hoping she would be the first with a tasty snippet. Little did she realise that she was often fed false stories for devilment.

Although there was still the dangerous situation to deal with, Russ always kept a close eye on his mother for reasons of his own. Denzil was aware of this and on the odd occasion he had done the observations for him just to throw any watchers off the scent, knowing they would be observed.

Even though Russ was in body at this time, he had the skill of going about his daily earthly routine but also work on the spiritual plane simultaneously, which proved he was on an extremely high level. He and Denzil had existed this way for a long time, with one or both being in body. Of course there were times when a particularly dangerous job had to be tackled, both were totally in spirit.

Violet was still feeling very uneasy, and although she couldn't pin it down to anything apart from her feelings near the empty house, she couldn't keep her mind on anything and she had the horrible sensation she was being watched. Just after lunchtime she decided to go out. She had heard of buildings having funny effects on people and thought a change of air couldn't do her any harm. Then the vicar's visit came back into her mind. Now what was all that about?

"I know. I'll go and see him." She decided.

Denzil had homed in on this with a very strong sense that this was wrong and did his best to turn her thoughts against it but she had made up her mind. It was decided that Russ would continue to monitor his mum as there was more to her just apparently digging for gossip, and Denzil would stay with Irene although the two friends would remain in close connection.

There are times when it seems a bit mean to let a person head into a possibly dangerous situation but you have to let them to gain information but try and afford them as much protection as possible without it being apparent to evil watchers.

Denzil knew Violet needed extra protection so immediately boosted her defences but only enough so as not to be detected. He was watching from a safe distance as she walked towards to vicarage. This was a modern house having been built at the same time as the little church and was on the same piece of land, but separated by a little gate set in a low hedge to give the impression that this part was private. On approaching the church she saw the old chap who kept the place tidy and cut the little bit of grass either side of the main gate.

"Hello Sam." She called.

He stopped and looked around to see who was calling.

"Oh hello there Mrs Trewicke, how are you?"

"Yes, I'm fine thank you, and yourself?"

"I keeps meself busy you know, best way to be."

She stopped.

"Um, do you happen to know if the vicar is in Sam?"

He stopped and looked at her.

"You be wanting him then?" He wasn't smiling now.

"Well, only if he isn't busy."

She was beginning to feel very uncomfortable as though this man was a guard and she was being examined. Denzil was aware there was more to this place than he thought.

"Mrs. Trewicke! How nice to see you again." The vicar's voice broke the tension and he came towards her with a smile which was very familiar, very different to the nervous look he had last night. But of course he was on his own ground now.

"Oh hello vicar, I just......" The words froze. It now seemed silly for her to even be here. How could she ask him what he had meant when he visited?

But Denzil wanted to know and gently pushed her toward the little gate which was now open for her to enter.

"Do come in, I think my wife has just made some tea."

What could she do? Her brain couldn't think of a sensible answer so with Denzil's help she went through the gate and followed the vicar to his house. Although she would later dismiss it as imagination, it was almost as though he had been waiting for her. She couldn't say she felt at ease and she would loved to have turned round and left at that moment.

She was led through the lounge into the conservatory where he indicated for her to sit. The tea was already on the table and she had the feeling she was expected. Seeing the two cups she asked politely if his wife was joining them but he said she was busy elsewhere and these were for them. It was a beautiful setting, the sun was on the lawn and the shrubs and the vicar was being very welcoming, so why did it feel wrong?

Denzil was on high alert now and warning Russ to watch for anything different near Irene for something sinister was at work but not showing its true colours. The atmosphere around the church area was what they described as 'too clean' which meant it had been specially sterilised on purpose to clear any traces of evil infiltration. It was often used in olden days after black magic or sacrifices so that no trace remained in the surrounding area and it is a thought that it has never actually stopped. This meant that the church or house was possibly being used for practices or just a base from which to operate.

This made Russ very alert and he exchanged a thought with his partner. What if the empty house was a decoy? It was very easy to give a certain feel to a place and as soon as the word spread people would soon elaborate and make up the rest themselves. But why had the vicar visited Violet and why was she now being drawn to the vicarage? There had to be more to it.

Warning bells went out. Denzil sent a team to Violet's for if she had been drawn away for a specific reason, it could be that evil was going to make placements in her home. Not only could she be monitored but controlled. In other words, she would be a tool to do their dirty work under the cloak of respectability. This was probably why she was drawn to the empty house. Then there was the question of Janet. Just how was she involved in all this? A guard would have to be posted near her to monitor her constantly for at this stage nobody could be trusted.

With their centuries of experience, neither Denzil nor Russ took anything for what it seemed. Of course they had to investigate anything unusual that was occurring but they also knew that truth was mixed with fiction and the skill was to separate the two. It is common knowledge that paranormal investigators come across some unexplainable happenings and however much they try to put a valid reason on something, there remains that element of doubt. For some things there are no answers.

At this moment the two friends were doing one of their summing up sessions. In the spirit world there are mischievous entities that will enter a building for instance, making sure they are detected. Then other people have to go and have a feel of the place, and they too would say "Oh yes, there's definitely a presence here." Before long, everyone with any claim to psychic powers has to go along and give their own view and soon the place is listed as haunted although the playful ones have long gone.

In some cases, people who are not so brave but are persuaded by their friends that they will have a fun time and it will be a blast, go under pressure but their nerves get the better of them and they imagine there are ghosts when in fact the place is deserted. Then there are the charlatans who, not wanting to loose face make up their own little stories.

Denzil had done a sweep of the corner house and grounds.

"Gone." He announced. "If there was anything there in the first place."

Russ was musing. "I'm more inclined to go for the false trail. But why did they want attention drawn to that place in particular."

"Custom made my friend." He paused. "Old empty house, hidden from the road, plenty of trees rustling in the dark. What could be better?"

"And so the story will go on that it's haunted." Russ's thoughts were racing.

"Auntie Vi has gone to the vicarage on an impulse."

"I think I know where you're going." Denzil was ahead of him. "And your mum, well Irene had such an impulse to go out gossip hunting this morning."

There was a deathly pause as they both had the same thought. Both ladies had been drawn away from their homes, believing it was of their own accord, but it left both houses empty.

"Quick, do a check on that Janet lady." Denzil almost shouted.

They both went to her home and like the others it was also empty.

At this point it was necessary to go into a special spiritual mode known only to higher levels. Clever evil sources can make even the spirit world see what they want, in fact they are experts at it and the two knew they weren't dealing with amateurs here.

All three abodes appeared perfectly normal apart from the usual visiting spirits going about their business. For a split second Denzil lifted to a high level, and when he was back Russ did the same, as they had to be careful not to leave any area completely unmanned at any time. The easiest way to explain this procedure is to imagine you have now acquired night vision so you are able to see what others can't but it is nevertheless there. They only had very limited time as they would soon be monitored by unwelcome sources if they stayed too long in any one place and could then be tracked.

Before most people could breathe in, the job was done and they divested themselves of the special powers and cleansed the areas they had visited. They now knew that a spirit sensor had been placed in all three homes but these were not for watching the ladies' movements, they were there for control. The two didn't need to question why the houses had to be empty, for they knew from experience that any resident, even a pet would pick up the presence and could frighten them away.

This led to another question. Who else had been targeted and indeed how many? Was it just coincidence that these were two of Russ's relatives plus the aunt's friend but could it be part of a much bigger picture.

"Denzil, I wonder if it's only females. We should be looking much further afield and ask our fellow operators what they know."

No sooner had the thought been exchanged that a plan was put into place. Of course it wasn't broadcast for all to see, that would have been rather obvious, but there were ways and means of getting the information secretly and quickly. Time is very different in the spirit world.

The answer was there immediately. Nobody outside of the town was affected and it seemed that the few that were known, were all female.

"Can't be random." Russ was feeling rather uneasy.

Denzil had picked up what his friend was now chewing over.

"One of the sites is yours."

The silence said it all. Was he the actual target?

The friends had dealt with many cases in the past and there was always the chance of some evil wanting to get even. A personal vendetta was often at the bottom of many an unusual event and few would know the reason as it could take decades, even centuries to appear. But someone, or something would want justice and not rest until it had been effected. Now it could be aimed at Russ or Denzil or most likely both of them. Although not uncommon, you always hoped it wouldn't happen to you, but in that line of work it was a strong possibility, but that couldn't stop you carrying on the fight against evil or the world including its surroundings would be at risk. And that would mean the whole universe as we know it.

The vicar had been talking to Violet about the flowers and the birds as though he didn't want a lull in the conversation but she sensed an uneasy feeling about him. Suddenly he put his cup down and turned in his chair to face her.

"I'm so glad you came."

"You are?"

"Well yes, you see you must have thought I behaved rather oddly but I wanted you to know that, well I'm always here if you want to talk about anything."

His look was quizzical as he studied her face and she felt he was looking right into her soul.

"Oh I would vicar, but there's nothing bothering me, nothing at all. Thank you for offering though. Very kind." She stood up.

He knew she wouldn't say any more and reluctantly saw her to the little gate.

As she walked home, her mind was racing with recent events but she was feeling quite refreshed in some ways and felt she would be alright now. As soon as she had got in and taken off her coat, she reached for the phone.

"Hello Janet. I thought I'd just tell you that I'm feeling so much better thank you. I've been to see the vicar and we had tea."

"Good." Her friend sounded pleased. "Well I think we can put the upset behind us now. I've walked past that house once or twice today and you'd never think there'd ever been anything creepy about it."

"Must be our age." Vi laughed.

"Depends which age you're talking about. Think we're a bit past the change by now!"

After a few more laughs the ladies hung up. Vi looked around the room. The atmosphere was different but not unpleasant and she knew everything would be alright from now on.

There was great consternation now as Denzil and Russ were considering their next move. It seemed it was necessary to form a bigger fighting force but to do that could ruin everything. They had noticed that groups of three people were forming, people that knew each other and hadn't been that close in the past but now had a connection. Also, when observed from above, these groups were forming a ring around the outskirts of the town.

Immediately they checked on other towns and cities nearby and the same thing seemed to be occurring but the size of the groups was relative to the size of the town or city. So although Riverbrook to use its local name, had groups of three, the nearest city had groups of nine and in larger towns it was six.

This had to be ominous. What was bewildering the pair now was how it had all happened so quickly without being noticed. They chastised themselves for concentrating on the smaller signs without thinking what else could be involved, but this was something different to the norm. It was as though a touch paper had been lit after the initial people were all in place.

Russ suddenly had a thought but Denzil was ahead of him and was on his way to Violet's. From a distance above they could see the link between her, Janet and the vicar's wife. So was that what the vicar was trying to warn her about? What came next was disturbing. They were looking for the other groups and Russ felt a cold spot below him. Together they saw it. The tie between Irene, Lily and the carer. The physical side of Russ felt sick but he knew more than ever now that they had to get to the bottom of it.

Trying to piece it together Denzil felt that these were not bad people, in fact in each set of three there was a church connection so was the evil trying to infiltrate various religions by getting inside them so as not to draw any attention to the real power behind it? It seemed obvious that the vicar at Vi's church had been aware of something very wrong and was trying to warn her. Also, either some good force had directed her to him, or the wife had drawn her there for some other reason. There were a lot of questions to be answered, and quickly.

They did a quick sweep of all other groups visible to them but the pattern was exactly the same so this was a very well planned operation and apart of knowing it had to be evil orientated, they knew no more. Also, it was possible that others would be springing up although the area seemed to be covered at evenly spaced points. Contrary to their initial thoughts, it was necessary now to direct teams to monitor all the other areas but it had to be covert. This meant they could give their full attention to this particular area, the one where Russ lived in body. He would need all his skills to carry on as normal when at home but that shouldn't be too difficult, he would keep on insulting his mother with various asides and hope she wouldn't get suspicious.

The thought had occurred to them that the people being used could have been primed to notice anything that could jeopardise the operation so he would have to form a sort of shield, but depending on how they were being monitored, the evil would soon spot it. It seemed that this called for every skill Russ could muster and he mustn't relax for a moment. Extra guards were called in to protect his bodily form when he was asleep but they too would have to merge into the background or they would raise awareness. Everything connected with this had to be top notch if they were to succeed.

Denzil decided to hover around the vicar's residence from time to time, not staying long and also he would monitor the empty house for it was easy to disregard something as soon as it appeared innocent, and that had been the downfall of many. Retracing of steps could hold the key to many things. Busy times ahead.

There are certain occasions when it is advisable, regardless of how proficient you are, to consult with your high angel contact. They have the knowledge of everything past, present and can also foresee what is to come. A bit like a spiritual encyclopaedia. Russ decided that while his twin was busy looking at the earthly connections, he would call upon a little extra help. The answer came before he had even time to make contact.

Immediately he called Denzil to do a special dot observation. This was an operation lower levels were of aware of but could not access. It had proved essential in many cases and hopefully now it would move this one forward.

The two moved themselves to a required distance from earth and concentrated. The groups of three were obvious by each one showing three blue dots, like markers on a map. Then they saw it. In the middle of each group was one red dot slightly larger than the others. Having got the information, they were back in their normal positions instantly.

This meant that a much stronger force was controlling and organising each group. Every single one would have to be under constant observation and the information spread around all the watchers. Experienced reinforcements were already in position to monitor the other groups around this town and any others affected. What had started like a small issue was becoming a massive threat to the area and alerts had to go out world wide to stem the spread. The problem was that this was only known spiritually so no one in body would have any idea of the danger that was lurking. Even those with religious leanings, ie vicars, ministers and regular church goers wouldn't know because the evil has ways of blocking anything they wish so the innocent folks carry on totally unaware of what is going on or how they are being used.

The other danger in these cases is the speed. One minute everything is ticking over nicely and the next, although unknown, is threatening every spirit's destiny whether still in an earthly body or working on the numerous spiritual planes. So nobody in whatever form is safe. Or so the evil would like to think. The heavenly powers are extremely strong and although may seem to be dormant, are in fact a fighting force who will stop at nothing to overcome any evil that threatens.

Chapter 4

When Russ returned home from work he tried to steer his thoughts away from the impending disaster. He wasn't sure just how much any members of the new groups would know and he didn't want to raise any suspicion so, as planned he would be his normal sarcastic self.

"Are you late?" Was the welcome he got.

"Here we go." He thought but answered "I don't know, am I?"

"I was asking you?" Irene hadn't turned to face him and kept her attention on the pots on the stove.

This didn't go unnoticed although he wasn't showing it. Normally she would be scrutinising him from head to toe. He decided to dangle a carrot.

"Well, in fact I was so fed up with work, I took the day off and went for a walk in the park."

She stopped for a moment then went on fussing over the vegetables.

"Oh well if you're in one of your silly moods."

He jumped straight in.

"And how was your visit?"

There was a hush.

"My visit? Nobody has been here. Nobody at all."

He paused before saying "Oh, sorry, my mistake, I thought you said you were going out today. Now who was it you were going to fleece for gossip?"

At least this was his normal attitude so she wouldn't pick up anything from it.

"Oh you mean Lily. Yes I went to see Lily. We had a nice chat, but I don't just go to be nosey you know. She doesn't get out and she's glad of the company. But she wouldn't have any gossip."

He was amused at the length of the explanation and it took him back to when he was a lad and had been caught doing something he shouldn't so overdid the excuses.

He kept fairly quiet while she was dishing up but when they were eating he popped the next question in, quite casually as though he was just making polite conversation.

"Poor soul. Having to rely on anyone that may go to see her. I mean what if nobody went?" He didn't look up.

"Well, that's how it is when you get old and can't look after yourself. I expect I'll be like that one day."

"So, she must be able to get washed and dressed and get something to eat for herself?"

He said it quite slowly knowing it would go in, and waited.

"Um, well, there is a carer goes in and keeps her clean."

"Oh that's good. How often?"

Just when it seemed to be going alright she put the brake on.

"Well, I've never known you to be so interested."

He had to think quickly.

"Just making conversation Mother. I thought you'd be glad that I'd at least remembered that you were going out. The rest is of no importance to me. Whether the old dear eats, sleeps, or has a shit."

"Russell!"

It must have gone deep for her to use his full name but shock treatment was needed to get him off the hook. It seemed to have worked judging by the tight lipped expression as she cleared the plates. He had restored his obnoxious image in a single word. The rest of the meal was pretty strained. He came in with the odd passing remark which was met with a 'hmm' but no words. Hopefully he had thrown her off any scent she may have thought she had.

Rosalie, the carer lived alone. She was about forty, divorced and her only daughter had got herself pregnant in her teens and left home. By now history had repeated itself and Rosalie was a grandma. She quite enjoyed her job as it meant she could meet people and she felt she was helping them. Some were not so easy to get on with but those such as Lily made up for it.

When she was on her way to her visit today, she had a strange feeling as she approached the house. Often she could pick up a vibe or a sensation but not always be certain as to whether it was good or bad. All she could say that was that something was different, not quite right. When Irene had arrived, it seemed to have become stronger and when she had left the house it faded, or so she thought. But the seed had been planted, and all three were now a group.

The question Russ had was who or what had done this. Denzil was inclined to think it had stemmed from one of them, rather than three being chosen.

"It might be an idea" suggested Russ, "to look at the groups and see if any one member has particular leanings. Say towards the occult or anything a bit off beat."

Denzil agreed but said "But looking at these three, none of them qualify."

"Just a minute, we've been blind. I've got to check something." And Russ was gone.

"Well?" Denzil had a feeling he knew what was coming as the other returned.

"The groups I've checked are all female."

There was a pause then Denzil went. He was back before you could blink.

"No. They aren't."

"What, but I've just done half the town."

Denzil paused then said. "And if you check the rest of the town they will all be female."

"So your point is?"

"The next town – the groups are all male."

They were both in thought as there was a definite pattern here. On checking, the town groups alternated, all female, all male, and so on. But the next question was the sex of the leaders. After a swoop they realised this was unknown, so they had to be of a much higher level or the twins would have been able to identify them. Help from another source was required so the request was sent.

While they were waiting the pair were trying to examine every small detail.

For example, were three targeted simultaneously, or was one selected then those who that one knew were added? In each case they looked at, each three did know each other although not necessary closely. No group was made up of three strangers.

"Wait a minute." Russ was on to something.

"Go on."

"Well, they didn't all know the other two. Yes, Vi, Janet and the vicars wife knew each other but look at mum. She knows Lily, and Lily knows the carer."

"But your mum didn't meet the carer until today. So she didn't know her before."

"But Lily knew them both." They chorused.

They were silence for a moment then Denzil said "I want to know more about the red dots."

"Yes, they are keeping them well cloaked. Are they known to the groups?"

"And the same sex? I've a feeling that is important although I don't know why."

Russ assured him "But we will, and I think it will be soon."

They were in thought for a moment then Russ said "Better go, she's calling up the stairs."

Irene was back in the kitchen when Russ appeared.

"Oh you made me jump, creeping up on a soul like that."

Russ couldn't resist it.

"Sign of a guilty conscience mother."

"What is? What are you gabbling on about?"

She certainly was very flushed and excitable so he decided to play on it.

"Have you seen the doctor lately? You are getting a lot of flushes you know."

"I'm alright, I've told you before so stop going on about it."

"Well, we wouldn't want you collapsing in church would we? Just how embarrassing would that be?"

"You are disrespectful, that's what you are. You make out you care but you don't give a fig."

"I think the word is 'toss' mother."

She was visibly shaking and he felt he had gone a bit too far but Denzil was watching closely and had noticed something.

There was something else with her, as well as her guardian, something else and he couldn't place it.
"What are you saying. You don't make sense." She was crumbling.
Russ wanted to stop but Denzil was pushing him to go on.
"The expression is you don't give a toss, or a flying fart." She left the tea she was making and hurried to the lounge where she flopped into a chair.
This was interesting. If something had taken her over, they must check on Lily and Rosalie quickly to see if there was any resemblance. Was it aggravation that had brought it to the fore?
In a way Russ felt guilty, he wasn't one to kick someone if they were down, but this was almost like something he had to do and maybe this is why he had to build up this wall of torment just to prepare for this moment. The mother he knew was almost lost in front of him, and it was as though he was looking at a stranger.
He went back into the kitchen, made the tea and brought it in. He needed to apologise but he knew he couldn't divulge the reason for his actions. He hoped that one day she would realise why he had been the way he had. But for now he must give her a little bit of comfort hoping they could stop whatever it was that was taking over her and so many more that were being used. Good people who wouldn't even know it was happening. But it had to be stopped before it had got a greater hold because then it would probably be too late.

Denzil had noticed something and drew Russ's attention to it once he had double checked. As Irene was half dozing in her chair, her son could give his twin all his attention for a moment.
"We know the town is surrounded by groups, but look again."
They were looking down on Riverbrook but gradually pulling back until the full picture emerged. There wasn't a random number, there were twelve sets each at the position of a clock face, to put it bluntly every one of them was on an exact map reference. Denzil had an uncontrollable habit of added numbers until he came down to a single figure.
"Twelve. One and two gives three."

As this was a usual practice Russ took little notice of it at first. But Denzil continued.

"Each group has three members. And there's something else."

"Go on." Russ was getting really interested now.

"It's changing all the time. Look at the groups."

Russ was wondering if he was imagining things and now realised that nothing was staying the same for long. Also it was apparent the movement wasn't to throw them off the scent, this was how it operated. The groups were now alternate male and female Vi was situated at six o'clock and Irene at 10 o'clock. So both were flanked by male groups, or so it appeared.

As they watched, Vi and Janet were both making their way to the vicarage and on arrival were greeted silently by the vicar who showed them into the conservatory where his wife was waiting, then he left them alone. To the onlooker not a word was exchanged. The three ladies sat with eyes closed and to the physical eye that was all there was. But the twins could see more and pulled back to get the full picture but they weren't expecting what came next. The red dot was centred over Sam who was now in the centre of the trio, not bodily but in spirit and he was directing vivid blue beams down, one to each lady. As quickly as it started, it was over. At that point the vicar came back into the room and showed the two visitors out in complete silence and he didn't even look at them. Vi and Janet walked without speaking and when they got to the spot where they went their separate ways, they merely gave a smile and went to their own homes.

Russ had followed them and noticed that as soon as they entered their own houses, they seemed to return to normal as though nothing had happened. Denzil had remained at the vicarage where it was a similar situation. The ladies left, the wife got up and went into lounge where she and her husband sat discussing other matters. But one thing intrigued him. Where did the vicar fit into all this? No normal person would act in that manner, so he must be party to it in some way, but what was it? That was something they needed to find out and quickly.

The two were back in conference immediately and Denzil came up with his next bit of information.

"Did you notice anything while the three ladies were being beamed?" He asked.

"Well I was concentrating on Sam, didn't expect him to be red dot. Such as?"

Denzil paused for effect.

"As these lights, beams or whatever they were, came down, the ones at 5 o'clock and four o'clock were also active. Don't worry they weren't that obvious in fact the ones at four were quite faint viewed from our position."

"So does that mean they are doing them threes, or were all done simultaneously?"

"As far as I can make out, one to three had already been taken care of. So then these three groups were beamed. So now I bet you seven to nine will be done, then….."

Russ finished it off "Ten, eleven and twelve. And Mum is at 10 o'clock."

"And you will be in the front line viewing position."

That hadn't crossed his mind.

"So she will have to go out! But I can't follow in body, and if I go in spirit she will know."

Denzil didn't seemed phased by it.

"I doubt if it will be immediately. There seems to be a gap between each of the three groups. Then he started musing. Three people per group. Three groups beamed at a time. Three times three is nine. Three times twelve is thirty six. Three plus six is nine. We need to know who is in the group at nine o'clock, or the red dot of that one."

Russ had listened patiently as he always did but had to ask.

"What is so special about the group at nine?"

"Because there has to be a controlling factor working within the operation, even hiding. Tell you what, while you are baby sitting your ma, I'll go and nose round any other places where this has happened, or something vaguely like it and see what I can dig out."

"Especially if there's a three or nine involved." Russ couldn't resist popping that in but the vibe he got told him that his twin was not amused.

Irene was snoring, her mouth wide open. She hadn't moved since their interchange and this seemed a good time for Russ to nip off spiritually and do a bit of digging himself. Although Denzil was of the highest intelligence and could come up with the answers most of the time, it could overshadow Russ's talents and now and then he liked to be let off the leash hoping he would prove he wasn't just an assistant but could work equally well alone, not that he would want it as a permanent state. His current objective was to see exactly what the vicar at Auntie Vi's church knew and why he didn't seem to be batting an eyelid at such strange goings on under his nose.

Not knowing quite what he would learn, he held back and viewed the vicarage from a distance. There was no sign of Sam and the vicar and his wife were watching television, and having cup of tea. All look so normal. Russ moved in a bit closer. Suddenly he was shot backwards and found himself back at home. What had pushed him away? He didn't have long to find out.

"What the hell did you think you were doing?" Denzil was angry.

"It was you. Why did you have to go and pull me out?"

"So that you didn't make a complete cock up of anything, or everything to put it bluntly. What possessed you to go nosing around?"

"Ha. I like that. Of course you don't."

"When I go nosing about as you put it, I don't just barge in and announce my presence. For your information I've wiped your wake that you so kindly left behind."

There was a stillness for some time then Denzil said "Look buddy, I have to be over cautious. I've got more than an instinct that this is something not big, not huge, but massive and I'm not sure that we are fully equipped to go blindly dashing in. We report to higher levels, ok?"

Russ had no option but to agree. It wasn't often they argued but he knew when his twin was right.

"So what to we do next?" he asked.

"Well, we do need to keep a distant view on when your mum etc are beamed and I mean distant, in fact I think we should let an independent watcher take that one. Perhaps safer if we keep right out of it."

"As long as we know straight away." Russ wanted reassurance.

"Don't worry, we'll be the first to know."

"Going on what you found out already, what sort of time are we looking at?"

Denzil paused. "Between first three and second three, only about an earth day."

"So going on that……"

"The next three, ie seven, eight and nine should be tomorrow."

"Making Mum the day after." Russ wasn't sure if he was relieved or not. Earth time can differ according to circumstance and in a way, he wanted it over and done with so he knew what they were up against. But that wouldn't be the end as the last three still had to be beamed.

Tuesday promised to be a bit nearer in temperature to what should be expected for summer so Irene thought she would take full advantage of it to get out of the house for a while. She was beginning to give up on hoping her son would mend his ways be and a bit more the way she had hoped he would be but as he got older he seemed to be getting more insolent. He'd been brought up very strictly but it hadn't seemed to have left any lasting impression. He'd been out with a few girls but always found fault with them but said he was still looking for the right one. His father had suggested when he was quite young, that he was on the other bus but she'd had to get him to explain that. The thought didn't sit well as she liked everything straight forward and her impression was that she hadn't brought him up like that.

But it was simply the fact that no female had been the right one and he hoped that one day some one would come along with whom he could be happy. Irene also didn't know just how involved he was spiritually. In her book if you didn't go to church, you were not a Christian, so not a good person.

Her mind went back to last Sunday and she had decided that there would be no repeat of that, for how could she hold up her head knowing people would be talking? But now she was still missing all the juicy gossip which seemed to have evaporated. It would be a tonic to find out a tasty snippet, especially against one of her churchgoers. Now that would make her day. But those that used to be the main spreaders had either moved into a home or just didn't confide in her any more.

There was little option but to give Lily another try. She was still peeved at having been 'told off' as she put it but something was urging her to go round and ignore any snide remarks. Little did she realise she had to go today and tomorrow and the decision was not of her making but she would be totally unaware of the group of three to which she now belonged.

As Lily sat waiting for Rosalie to come, she half expected 'nosey knickers' to make another appearance for the seed had been planted in her mind. The burning question in the twins' thoughts was 'what was the identity of the red dot?' as there seemed to be nobody else connected with these ladies. Obviously someone was yet to enter the equation but there wasn't much time, in fact only until the next day. Denzil certainly wasn't going to be far away on this one.

The doorbell went. Lily reached for the handset that showed her who was at her door. It was her, the nose.

"Just a minute." She said into the handset.

"Take your time."

Why did the tone always seem so patronising?

She didn't hurry and let Irene in.

"I'm expecting Rosy." She said without turning as she made her way back to the lounge.

"Oh. Who's Rosy?

Lily wasn't hurrying on purpose and she felt the woman's frustration at having to go at such a slow pace.

"My carer. You saw her last time. It's not her name but it's what I call her."

"Oh her. Yes. I remember."

When they were seated she wasted no time.

"So, how have you been?"

Lily didn't hurry with a reply. She was setting the pace and getting a fiendish delight out of it.

"Since yesterday you mean?"

"Oh, is that all it was? I don't know where my brain is at the moment, and that son of mine doesn't help. In a world of his own most of the time." She ended with a laugh which was quite unnecessary.

"Yes, I think you said that before."

If Lily sounded bored, that was exactly how she intended. She'd like this woman to go, but somehow she knew that wasn't going to happen although she had no idea why.

"Well I don't have much news I'm afraid, there isn't much of any interest going on to tell you about." Irene was on the point of concocting something to see if that brought Lily out, when the door bell went again.

"That'll be Rosy, do you want to let her in for me?" Lily purposely didn't add 'please' as she knew that the omission would rattle Irene's cage and she got a naughty little tweak of pleasure from it.

"Well alright. As I say, anything I can do, you only have to ask." But added in her mind "but a few manners wouldn't go amiss."

As she opened the door Rosalie came in followed by a younger woman. Irene looked at them both as if she was waiting for an explanation as to who the other one was but none came so she had no option but to close the door and follow them into the room.

"Hello Lily, this is Lisa she's training with us. Are you happy for her to be here?" Rosalie indicated for the new girl to come forward but this still left Irene in the background which didn't go down well.

"And I'm her friend, I come round to see if she needs any shopping." Irene's voice got through where her body couldn't.

Lily completely ignored it as did the others, and spoke to Lisa.

"Lovely to meet you my dear and you are very welcome." Then she almost whispered "We all have to learn, don't we?"

Rosalie looked very pointedly at Irene almost telling her, without words that she was not needed for the lady's privacy, but this woman wasn't taking the hint so direct measure were needed.

"Um, as it's a bit crowded today, would it be better if you could call at another time?"

The tone wasn't exactly a request and Lily was loving every minute of it.

"Well, I …won't get in your way alright?"

What came next was unexpected.

Rosalie faced her and said very slowly "In this job, our main objective is the dignity of the service user, that is the person receiving care and with two of us here to attend to Lily, in order to keep this, it wouldn't be very professional of me to allow you to stay would it? Now, with Lily's permission, if you want to be really helpful, why don't you go to the kitchen, do any washing up and make her a nice drink, and when she has been washed and dressed, you may return."

You could have cut the air with a knife and Lily was biting her lip so as not to smile.

"Is that ok Lily?" Rosalie was asking.

"Oh yes, that's absolutely perfect. You may do as she says." She called over to Irene who was not best impressed but at least she was still here and who knows what she may pick up if she kept her ears open?

Denzil knew exactly why she had to remain. This was a trial run, for the red dot was positioned over Lisa. The four were complete and ready for the three to be beamed. Russ had witnessed this by remote and was eager to hear what excuse his mum would make for visiting the next day, that is if she even told him.

Although Russ could carry on his daily job and still be in touch spiritually, he was always glad when he could relax and converse with Denzil to have a proper exchange and make sure he hadn't missed anything. Lunchtime seemed to take ages to arrive but as he sat, apparently reading a magazine, he was in full conference.

"Well," Denzil was quick to bring him up to speed, "that was quicker than I thought, the cells certainly aren't hanging around."

"Hmm."

"You don't seem very enlightened. You did get a view of Lisa?"

"Oh yes, it isn't that. I think it might be better if we conversed later when I don't stand any chance of being distracted."

Denzil sensed trouble. He'd seen Russ act this way before and it meant he was probably going off at a tangent and not concentrating on the enormity of the task in hand. Trying to see if he could draw him out at this stage he jokingly said "Oh, you did see her. Like her did you?"

"Of course not, I mean yes she was very nice but I only got a glimpse."

Denzil kept pushing, but instinct told him this was nothing to do with Russ's mood.

"Well you had better be there when she comes again."

"Oh I don't mean, not like that."

Russ was obviously unnerved by something and he had to find out what it was and without delay.

"As soon as you've had your dinner, no, change that, I'll be there when you get home. Got some things to check out."

And he was gone or so Russ thought. In fact Denzil was going to be observing his twin very closely and that didn't mean he had to be anywhere in the vicinity for he could distance watch without even those close to him knowing.

The afternoon may have dragged for Russ but elsewhere there was quite a bit of activity. There was no secret in the fact that Vi and Janet were going to make their visit to the vicarage a daily routine. Each time the same thing would happen. Sam would raise his cap as they arrived then apparently get on with his work, the vicar showed them into the conservatory then left. At almost a given point he would return and show the two out. The three ladies would receive the beams in silence, neither of them reacting but just remaining perfectly still. The question still remained, what was the vicar's part in all this? He was obviously privy to it but in his position in the church surely this was strange.

Comparing this with the group Irene was involved in, there was nobody there in the vicar's role, that is, only the four appeared to be in presence and was it significant? But one thing was strange. Irene had gone thinking she would gather some tasty gossip which seemed to be foremost in her mind. Lily couldn't stand her and with her temperament could easily tell her to clear off. Rosalie was doing her job and apparently had no idea of anything spiritual going on. Now Lisa had made an appearance and still nothing seemed obvious to them. Just day to day work.

It seemed strange that not one of them had given the slightest indication of being in a special group.

On examining the other groups in this clock formation Denzil found the same thing, in fact it was quite a mixed bag. Some would start with more, then dwindle off until only the four remained. Others were very much closed groups and wouldn't entertain the thought of anyone else infiltrating them. But there was one common similarity. They all met at one of the member's homes, and always the same one. That must mean something and it had to do with the positioning of the blue beams.

Chapter 5

Russ was very quiet when he came home and Irene wondered if he was sickening for something. It was always her reaction if he went into himself and she sometimes even wished he'd turn round and be his rude self. It wasn't like him to let his spiritual work merge into his physical but there were occasions when something was so demanding or needed a lot of mental sorting that he had to switch off.

"I popped in to see if Lily was alright again. She's not good you know." She looked at him to gauge his response.

"Oh. Is she poorly then?"

"I told you, she can't wash herself now, the carer goes in every day. I hope I never get like that."

"So do I." Went through his mind but he said "That's sad isn't it."

"Well it is. You work all your life then it has to come to this."

"To what?" His mind had wandered already.

Irene stopped folding some things she was going to iron.

"I think you should see the doctor. You aren't yourself and you know what that means."

"I'm alright Mum. Just been very busy at work and my mind just needs to wind down a bit."

"Well….."

"Tell you what, I'll have an early night, that usually puts me back on my feet again."

"If you like but I shall be keeping an eye on you my lad."

What was really going through her mind was that if he was at home ill, it may hamper her going to Lily's. For some reason she never questioned the fact that she must go every day, and her mind had been programmed to believe it was for Lily's benefit.

Denzil was waiting for him and he seemed concerned.

"Ok. Out with it. You are harbouring something. What is it?"

"I don't know how to start, I mean how to put it. It won't sound right."

There was a pause before Denzil offered "What if I said I've been waiting for you to broach it?"

"But you don't know – I mean – how could you?"

"You know your thoughts are not your own. I pick up on everything."

"But I cloaked this, until I was ready?"

"So, you are ready. Go for it."

Russ took a deep physical breath.

"It's been going round in my mind. When the twelve positions in this area were formed, they were all female. And the ones in the next town to them were all male. Now these are alternated and so are the others. I checked."

"And you want to know how and when and probably why they did change places."

"Well, yes. It's not a daft question surely."

Denzil drew him to a position above Vi's group.

"Take a close look at the ones on either side."

"Yes I see, they are male."

"What makes you say that?" Denzil had the appearance of a knowing smirk.

"Well I can see."

"But before you said they were female."

"Well the original ones were, before the swap."

"But there was no swap.

This is where the difference in spiritual levels of the two was obvious and needed explanation.

Denzel moved them well away as they didn't need to be in this area for him to make it clear to Russ just what was going on.

"Every single person was specifically placed for a reason. Balance. As you know in the higher spiritual planes we are sexless. For those in body and those in the lower levels gender is important, but not everyone is in the body they would wish.

Some are trapped. For example, the group to the left of Vi have female bodies, but they are male orientated. Now apply that to the other five similar groups in that clock formation."

Russ was trying to piece this together.

"So they are all in female bodies but half of them are basically men."

"Correct and before you ask, we are only seeing them in their true selves now because of the beams."

There was a moment's pause before Russ completed the format.

"And where we thought they were all male, half of those were in truth women, inside. And the beams have shown this."

"And so…" Denzil knew it was becoming obvious now.

"Nobody changed places!" Russ almost shouted the thought.

"No. They are all being who they want to be, for a while" Denzil added "until they reach a high enough level to be neutral."

After a moment Russ said "There is no distinction in the upper levels so why is it so important lower down?"

Denzil let him ponder to work it out for himself. It only took a minute.

"Of course. Physical procreation. It's needed for all physical species to continue but it is not required in the spiritual as no new life is being created, only recycled."

"Well I don't know if some of the hierarchy would put it quite like that but you have the drift. But there is another factor which is not widely discussed."

"Oh?" Russ was hooked now.

"Well, before we go into that, let us just come back to one factor about the different sex situation."

"Oh there's more?" Russ laughed thinking "now what's he going to surprise me with?"

Denzil was serious now.

"Take a look at yourself."

"Excuse me!" Russ didn't expect that.

"In what category would you put yourself?"

"What is this? I'm male. No doubt about that."

"You certain of that are you? When did you last have a girl friend? Are you still a virgin?"

"Now hang on. There's no doubt about my leanings."

Denzil did a retrace of previous lives.

"Here you were a girl with no interest in boys. Next you were a boy, but hated girls. And so on. Now you are neither, sexless."

"I like women. I can fancy a tasty piece when I see one, but I never come across one that really turns me on."

Denzil had to ask.

"And what about men?"

"What about them?" Russ was getting really steamed up by now.

"They don't appeal to you?"

"No they don't. Hey what are you implying?"

"Calm down. Basically you have no leanings either way and that indicates that some of your identity knowledge is blocked for a reason so you can live this life out without any ties, and then take your proper place."

"And you were put here to be my guardian."

"That's about it. It was always going to be a shock but you would have to have learned soon anyway."

There was quite a long pause. This kind of information would be a shock to anyone and Russ was realising that he was about to embark on the most demanding journey of his life.

"Can I ask, well maybe you wouldn't know but….."

"Go on."

"If I'm so high up, why am I having to live this earthly life? Surely I would have achieved the position long ago?"

"I'm not supposed to tell you."

"But you must."

"It could put you in danger, and you will know soon, so please don't ask any more at this time."

They had a few moments to adjust then Denzil said that Russ must return to his body.

"But I still don't know the purpose of the clock formation. I suppose you know what that is as well."

"Possibly." Was all he was going to get on that subject.

It was only when he felt alone he realised that Denzil hadn't told him what the other matter was that wasn't supposed to be discussed. Maybe he had been fobbed off and would never know.

"Well we'll see about that." He mused. "If I am from such high realms, maybe I will get to learn more than my teacher."

Rosalie had been uncomfortable the moment Lisa joined the carers group. It was a private company but often used to help out if the demand was great elsewhere. They got to know who worked for whom and more importantly who were the dedicated workers and those who simply took anything because they needed the money. The ones they despised were those offloaded by the social security who insisted they got a job or they would lose their benefits. They didn't usually stay long and flitted from one place to another not really wanting to work.

But Lisa was just the opposite. Far from being a passenger she had tried to take over right from the start. The experienced carers who knew everything about those in their charge, resented being told what to do and how to do it by some little upstart. Although they tried not to show their annoyance in front of their clients, some were quick to pick up the vibes and Lily for one never missed a trick. She hoped the girl wouldn't be in tow the next time and she could crawl round Rosy and find out what was going off. And if she spiced it up a bit she could feed that so call friend of hers a tale to make her socks go up and down. Oh yes, she could have a bit of fun here.

Not guessing what was in store for her, Irene was getting withdrawal symptoms. Didn't anybody know anything these days? A while ago, one could stand at their front door and find out anything, from what was going on two doors away to what was happening all over the world, not that she was particularly interested that far afield. She wanted to know who was living where they shouldn't, who'd got the sack, who was up the duff and important things like that.

She went to church regularly and prayed for the poor and sick, but wouldn't have given a penny to help them. In fact she was the most two faced hypocrite imaginable yet would be the first to criticise anyone else. The face she put on to the world was a far cry from what she was inside, but what she didn't realise was that people could see straight through her. They didn't like her, they merely tolerated her but wished she would go and worry somebody else. No wonder her son didn't go out with her.

That's why a few heads turned when Russ had gone to matins with her previously. Even the non gossips turned that one over in their minds. There were a few who had worked it out and exchanged a few choice comments.

"Well I think he did it just to annoy her."

"Did you see his face? He was taking the mick."
"I think he wanted to show her up for what she is."
"He's such a nice lad. Never married though."
"Ha, who'd want her for a mother in law?"

Of course, there were plenty of the other kind of comments, some not to pleasant, and in some cases well spiced with a few unprintable words.

Those in high places often pull the strings to make their puppets perform and this was no exception. Although related by marriage, Violet and Irene had no blood tie so spiritually were independent and it seemed to Russ that it was a coincidence that they were in these groups at this particular time. Obviously they wouldn't be in the same one geographically but they were oblivious to what they were both part of. Also, there was a different level of how they went about it. Violet and Janet went without question to the vicarage at the same time each day but why would anybody do that without a specific reason, then go home as if nothing had happened? Irene of course thought she was gossip harvesting but when that hit a blank she still went to Lily's and would continue to do so.

Russ knew he had to study the other groups in the clock in the hopes of getting an answer. At this point Denzil cut into his thoughts.

"Why not look closer to home first?"

"I'm not with you."

"Why look at others when you haven't studied these in detail yet?"

"Are you trying to tell me they are all identical in some way.?"

Denzil wanted to sigh but instead tried to make it simple.

"In each of these two groups, you know two of the people. Violet and Janet. Irene and Lily. But you don't know Sam, Janet, Rosalie or Lisa. Wouldn't it be wiser to find out where all these fit in first rather than wander round ten other groups of strangers? Then when you have found out all you can here, that is the time to extend your feelers."

There was a very significant pause and the air was trembling. Russ wanted his answer to come out as he meant it without any chance of inuendo.

"I keep getting this very strong feeling that you know all the answers already, and you are merely testing me to see how I perform."

"No, I don't know all the answers. I am here to guide you but you must realise that you do have to work everything out to progress."

That word set off an alarm bell.

"Progress to what?"

There was silence. Denzil let Russ have enough time to try and realise the full extent of his task although he would only learn one stage at a time before moving on to the next.

"Ok. So I study each of these two groups, thoroughly. Then what? Do I go round and check all the others to see if they are all doing exactly the same thing? And another thing."

"Go on."

"What is the time factor? We can see the groups building with three blue and one red which we think is a controller. Some aren't fully formed but are all going the same route. And the speed that this has grown from nothing means - well - I don't think it will take that much longer to be complete."

Denzil gave it a moment before coming out with his next thought.

"And what has it got to do with you?"

"What?"

"You've never seen anything like this before, but believe me it goes on quite often."

"Well thank you."

Denzil laughed.

"Sorry to burst your bubble. Listen, you have not been privy to witness this before but it is no threat, no evil force behind it but, and I mean a big but, it has to be protected against evil. Those involved will be very vulnerable while they are taking part."

Russ was stunned.

"It's some sort of ritual?"

Denzil wanted to stem the questions and slow him for now.

"Look, do what we just said. Go and find out more about the ones in the two groups, don't look further, there is no need."

"But why can't you tell me more? Just come out with it. You know what I will find so why waste time?"

"Because you have to learn and you have to find it out for yourself."

They were still for a while.

"I want to know why they have a controller," Russ said "and also, who gives them their instructions? The three get beamed, but the controller doesn't. That has to mean something."

Denzil was slightly amused.

"As long as you are coming in from the right angle."

"What?"

"Think about it. Don't just go for the obvious."

The session was at an end and Russ felt as if he was more in the dark now than before. His friend's words were making him stop and wonder. Had he been so wrong? What angle? He decided to put it completely out of his mind and then come back with a fresh approach after a while, but somehow everything wouldn't leave him and he had to solve this.

Downstairs Irene was thinking of going to bed where she could lie and muse over what time she would go to Lily's tomorrow to have some time to chat without those other two being there ordering her about. There was something about the young one she didn't like. It was almost as though she could see right through her and as for that Rosy, or whatever her name was, she could get off her high horse and stop throwing her weight about. Who did she think she was? Well, she'd teach her a thing or too. But that was tomorrow.

Russ had slipped into a dream state although he felt he wasn't properly asleep. He was looking over a green meadow where sheep were grazing when he realised they weren't just dotted here and there, they were in a pattern. In threes. His senses sprang into action and as he watched they began to move towards him, still in threes but they formed a straight line across the field, all facing him. This was a bit unnerving and he tried to pull himself fully awake, but he seemed trapped in this floating state and couldn't do anything about it.

Then the sheep had gone and he was looked over the whole meadow again but this time there were cows in groups of three all brown and white. Then he saw other cows that were black and white which seemed to be apart from the rest. As he watched the brown and white cows came towards him in threes but then something happened that made his blood run cold. The black and white ones joined them but in each group one black stood in the middle of three brown. Then the brown ones lay down leaving the black standing. He was transfixed. Then as if on cue, a beam of red light came down over the black cows and they vanished. In a split second, the brown and white ones were grazing randomly as though nothing had happened.

He was awake now and Denzil was watching him.

"Well? What did that tell you?"

It took a minute for Russ to be able to settle himself, let alone translate his dream into reality.

"That was so weird. But was it telling me that although the blue dots are being beamed now, that it's the commanders who will be....?" he was searching for the right explanation "…..taken, transported, removed or whatever this is building up to?"

"Well you are certainly on the right track. Remember, you have to look at it from the right angle."

"There's something else I would like to check because I don't suppose you will tell me."

"You're learning." Denzil laughed. "I am merely your guide, your mentor, but whether you pass your exams is up to you. But go ahead, I'll be interested in what you find."

Russ was getting the feeling constantly now that his friend knew all the answers but was having to make him do all the work to prove his worth. In a second he found what he wanted and was back.

"Well?"

Russ paused.

"You know very well but I will say. Because Vi's group have a passenger, ie the vicar, and Mum's doesn't…"

"You checked out all the others." Denzil finished it off for him.

"Do you want me to explain?" The tone of the thought was loaded with sarcasm.

"Please do."

"Instead of a clock, think compass. The north, east, south and west positions all have the extra one but none of the others."

"Go on. What word did I tell you was significant?"

"Balance." Russ almost shouted. "They are stabilizers, not part of the actual operation but they are essential."

"Spot on. They are all very strong spirits and are used regularly for this kind of…." he paused "….job."

Russ would like to have asked what was meant by that, but he was learning that he could only find out as factors fell into place and couldn't jump over anything to the next stage. That was why Denzil was there as his guide.

"Can I ask though, do they remember after, whatever it is, what they were doing?"

"That is not important. Don't concern yourself with that side of it. Concentrate on the ultimate result."

Although he didn't voice his thoughts, Russ thought this strange. Up to now he had been advised to leave no stone unturned in his quest to learn, even the smallest piece of information could prove vital in later stages, so why was his friend glossing over this particular aspect? No doubt he would have the answer sometime.

Janet had been feeling a bit different recently but couldn't explain it. She didn't feel ill or even under the weather. There was nothing in her life to get her excited as the family didn't live near so she didn't go on shopping sprees or birthday parties and most of her socialising was at church. She took an active part in any function even if it was making the tea, and being of a charitable nature would willingly help if anyone was in trouble or sick. She had almost forgotten the empty house incident and although she made her daily visits to the vicarage, the strange thing was that she didn't know why and also didn't question it. It was almost like a ritual. Nobody spoke or looked at each other apart from a greeting as they arrived and a nod as they left. It was strictly business, no cup of tea, no chatting, yet this still didn't raise any questions in her mind. It was almost as though it was something that she was programmed to do. Although she was friendly with Violet, they didn't go as friends but as single items which would make up a whole unit.

Even Violet didn't query this sudden change in circumstances but it was something that had to be done regardless of anything else in her life. What neither of them knew was that fate would make sure they attended and if anything threatened, it would be dealt with.

It was noticeable that although all twelve sectors were operating, they were not all going at the same pace. For instance Violet and Janet's group were slightly ahead of Irene and Lily's but this was often the case. What was important was that when all were in position, things would move forward. Several had started with only the blue dots and the red arrived when ready but it was gathering momentum almost like a wheel that starts spinning and you can see every bit of it, but as the speed increases it becomes a blur.

Russ had left for work but his spiritual side was very much in tune to learn of the progression of his mother's group now Lisa had appeared. Being Wednesday, he wondered if the days of the week had any bearing on the activities of the various groups. His aunt and mum went to church on Sundays so did that make any difference to this particular operation? If others didn't have any religious leanings, would that affect anything? This seemed to be a spiritual thing but all good people didn't necessarily go and worship with others on one particular day. Some could be working in hospitals tending the sick. Surely that was because they were caring people putting others before themselves. Did you have to kneel down in a building to pray?

Denzil was hovering so he took advantage of asking the question.

"Just how much is religion playing in all this?"

The reply made him stop what he was doing because it was so obvious.

"Everyone has a soul."

"Of course. But that means this whole thing is related just to the soul not what anyone does at work or worship, or anything."

Denzil explained.

"Because you saw one group meet at a vicarage, you assumed it had to be related to the church. Take a moment to look at all the other groups."

It only took an instant to realise that this was a totally random selection and it didn't apply to what they did, but where they were in other realms. In the physical we take death for granted, it happens all the time and we are sad because we will miss the one that has departed. But they are still in spirit somewhere, although that also has a time limit depending on so many factors.

To put it simply. If a person has been born into the physical for however many lives they need and acquired all the spiritual knowledge required for them to move on, they ascend to a higher plane. It is thought that we use seven earth lives, but in many cases they are not required so are very short lived however tragic that may be for the parents. But the spiritual is not just recycling souls indefinitely. What may take centuries in earth measurement is totally different in the spirit world where time can be shorter or longer or even endless.

And so we come to the ultimate move, the reason for the clock formation.

Denzil would let things progress so that Russ could learn from experience what was about to happen. All the dot positions had to be filled and with the arrival of Lisa, they were now complete. The four stabilisers were checked and solid. There was one final move to complete the process.

The day seemed endless, and when at last Russ got home he was very agitated for he knew something was about to happen but Denzil hadn't explained what it would be.

"I've got to pop round to Lily's again this evening." Irene didn't look at him as she dished up the dinner.

"Oh, isn't she well?" Russ knew why she was going but wondered if the poor thing even realised herself.

"No, she's alright but I had to do a bit of shopping for her and she's a bit lonely and what with her leg and that."

Russ couldn't remember if she had a bad leg or anything else and he wasn't really bothered. It was the fact she was going.

"Um will you be able to get in ok?"

"Oh she's lent me a key. Her carer has one as well. Saves her getting up all the time."

"Oh yes it would I expect. Does that other one go?"

Irene stopped.

"Other one?"

"Oh I thought you said there were two now."

Irene paused for a minute. He seemed a bit more interested than usual and she wondered what he was up to.

"Oh only a trainee." She fobbed it off.

"Well be careful. Perhaps I had better run you round in the car."

They were eating now and she looked as though she was thinking before answering.

"Well alright. Might be better. I know it's light till late but I'm not sure what time I'll be coming back."

"I'll bet you don't." He thought to himself but said "Well you can ring when you are ready and I'll come then."

"Being a bit considerate for a change." She muttered.

He came back in the same tone with "Can't do anything right."

They didn't have much more to say during the meal and when they had cleared away and washed up she said "Do you want a cup of tea?"

"No thanks, I'll have one when I get back."

When she was ready he drove her to Lily's and was waiting for her to get her key in the lock and go safely inside when the door opened and Rosalie beckoned her in.

"Must have seen her coming." He thought but knew there was more to this than was obvious.

He couldn't wait to get home where he could converse with Denzil without interruption.

"Well, she didn't hide that very well." His friend said.

"No, I'd have thought she'd have been much more covert."

But Denzil reminded him "They are almost programmed and they must carry on whatever."

"You aren't new to this are you? You know exactly what is coming next."

"It's essential for as long as I have the job."

Russ thought.

"Do you mean this is all you do?"

"Pretty much."

"For how long?"

Denzil gave a spiritual laugh.

"Now that is a question I can't answer."

They were silent for a moment then Russ said "Are you going to let me in on the next step because something is happening tonight isn't it?"

"It is."

Before he had chance to ask any more, Denzil beckoned him to a position above the clock.

"Notice anything?"

Russ looked around all the sections. The blues were all in position and the reds were in the middle of each.

"Don't think I do."

"What's missing from the clock?"

Russ looked again. Everything with still in place. Then he realised what his friend meant.

"The hands? Clocks have hands. But this one doesn't, wait, there is a second hand and it is going round very slowly."

"What else?"

As nothing else seemed to have changed Denzil told him to watch the centre. It seemed to have a smudge appearing which started to change colour until it settled as a vivid purple.

"What's that?" Russ was transfixed now. He hadn't noticed that all the blue dots had beams coming down and the red dots had red beams directed to them.

"It is when a spirit is recalled." Denzil was saying. Everything here is to give the absolute protection for such an important transition. Nothing must affect it."

"Oh I see. But who's spirit?"

The reply was almost inaudible.

"Yours."

"What?" Russ could feel his whole self being gently pulled towards the centre and Denzil's voice was getting fainter.

"You will learn more when you arrive. Farewell my friend."

As the second hand reached twelve o'clock, a vivid purple beam descended on the central spot and Russ had left. All he was aware of was the shock wave. If only he had been prepared for this but the words were echoing through his entire being.

"Your spirit has been recalled."

"Wake up. Wake up. You'll be late for work."

The sound of Irene's voice was almost a relief.

"What? I must have been dreaming." He slowly opened his eyes.

"You had me worried there my lad. Never known you to sleep so sound. Thought you'd passed out I did."

"What time is it Mum?" He sat up now.

"Nearly half past. There's a cup of tea ready so just gather yourself together."

As she turned to leave the room a very worried look was on her face. She thought he had been screaming in the night as though he was having a bad dream.

"That's what it was," she muttered as she got down the stairs, "he's had a nightmare. Hope he's not sickening for something."

But it hadn't been a dream as he was about to find out.

Chapter 6

Russ couldn't wait to make contact with Denzil because nothing was making sense. He could remember very vividly the clock formation, the lights and the realisation that it was he who was having his spirit recalled which came as an indescribable shock. So why did he wake up in his own bed the following day? But had he? His mind was trying to compute everything into a logical pattern but he kept hitting a brick wall and it was making him angry especially towards his friend who obviously had all the answers. But where was he? Normally he would have been there waiting for him to get up so they could discuss everything. Russ's guardian angel moved close to him and on a breath of air said "He has gone."

"Gone? Gone where?" Then as an afterthought "Was it all a trick?"

"Far from it." The tone was getting stronger now.

"I need to know everything." Russ was having a wash but his mind was not on work and he wasn't satisfied with the next message.

"You must live today as normal and let everything calm in your mind, then when you come home, all will be explained."

"But….." He didn't finish as he knew it would be to no avail. The day would be a long one especially as he wouldn't have his friend to converse with.

"Friend. Ha." He was angry until another thought hit him. "Oh my god!"

Something could have happened to Denzil spiritually. In his work he was always at risk, often a sitting target but he managed to survive due to his experience. But not being able to contact him was almost like a death. He missed him already and something told him nothing would ever be the same again. It was a very sobering thought but he had no choice but to do as his guardian said and ride out the day as best as he could. He wasn't even sure that he wanted to hear more but knew that he must for his own sanity.

If Russ was surprised at the outcome of the previous night, it was nothing compared to what Denzil was now adjusting to. As soon as the purple beam appeared it masked another of a colour only witnessed in the spiritual world, and this was the one to transport him, for it he was the one who's spirit had been recalled.

This can not be explained in earthly terms and has to be viewed from a totally different aspect but then it is very hard to understand until you are in that position. Some find it very difficult and don't come to terms with it but some of those more spiritually aware may see more than they expect.

What was not apparent to either of the two friends was this. When a person/spirit is earth connected, they are not always using their own free will. Of course that is a big part of how you live your life and you do have a control, but overall you are still under the influence of the hierarchy.

Russ was a very high arch angel, but to carry out his current task, it was necessary to wipe or delay his memory of his true self. There were several reasons for this but mainly for his protection for there were many evil forces at work who would try and waylay him and either drain his powers and knowledge or hitch a ride to find out what the good forces were up to.

Denzil was also very high up and believed his task was to see his friend safely delivered when his spirit was recalled, little knowing it was his turn. But this subterfuge was essential, for if even a fleeting thought had entered either of their minds, it would be monitored and all would be lost. So the powers above reversed the roles. Denzil believed from the start that he had to prepare his friend who didn't seem to be catching on very quickly at times, but that was just what was required. Even at the very last milli second Denzil still didn't realise it was his spirit's departure that he had been working towards.

As we know, time is very different when away from the earth and it would take a while for him to adjust. He had been placed in a very secure zone known to only a few and would have to learn what recall actually meant, for it wasn't just a removal from the earth, it was much more than that.

It was part of the plan that Russ stayed in earth form for a while because if he had returned to his normal plane, not only would evil entities work out a format for future recalls so they could intercept souls on their final journey, but his true identity would be revealed and the high levels wanted him to appear as an insignificant tool to be used at will, but carry no threat. How long that would last would have to be seen and a close eye would be kept on him from afar.

Denzil was aware that he was somewhere strange but he had been given the equivalent of a sedative, but in spiritual terms. This was for the same reason that Russ was being kept a bit in the dark, for spiritual wave patterns can be intercepted and at a time like this there would be many who wanted to gloat that they were the first to pick up on the operation and how it had been carried out. So it had to be played down from every aspect.

He questioned if he was near the earth but there was no reply. No matter how he tried to imagine his surroundings, it was no good. Although he had lived several earth lives and experienced the transition of passing back into spirit at each death, this was different.

The best way to describe it is like this. Imagine you have passed out. After the first moment of absolutely nothing, you start to hear. Then it's as though little boxes containing different places are spinning round for you to pick the one you were in before you became unconscious and you can't be fully return until you get the right one. Very unpleasant, especially for someone who faints a lot.

"Where am I?" He asked several times but still no answer so he drifted off again.

What he didn't know was that he was never in one place for more than about half a second and not only was he being moved, but was nowhere near even the solar system. Had he known, it would have been an even greater shock but the existence he was now entering cannot be compared to anything in terms as we know it.

The question that must spring to mind is – what will happen to the groups?

Simply nothing, as if they never existed. The people involved were picked from those that could just have their little meetings without anyone noticing. They all formed the strong clock formation which was needed for protection from all angles but it would be wiped from their memories and they would carry on as if nothing had happened. At the precise second when the actual recall was made, they were replaced with much stronger elements and allowed to leave for their own safety, their job completed. Would they be used again? Who knows? It is not for anyone in body or total spirit to question the movements of their high angels. It is also a guarded secret as to how many and when spirits are recalled, but it is surmised that when once you are gone, it is final. Where you go or what you do, no one knows. One fact does seem obvious. The ones that are recalled are already in total spirit and have no living relatives on earth so that their transition has no effect upon friends or loved ones. This is why it seemed strange to Denzil that Russ should be selected but he knew if he asked there would be no answer. But before long he would get more answers than he bargained for.

Irene was back to wanting her gossip but her sources were getting less and less. Didn't anyone do anything a bit naughty these days? Her neighbour seemed to give her a wide berth and the corner shops weren't what they used to be. Now there was a good source of regular news, but the shopkeepers she knew had all left and the new ones just wanted to take your money.

"Oh well I'd better go and check on Lily, but not when those women are there."

She made up her mind to go a bit later and get her on her own, then she might be alright, regardless of how Lily pretended there was nothing to tell. Probably just for show anyway. The trouble was that these days with all the laxity of morals, gossip just wasn't what it was. When she was young, if a girl had got herself pregnant she would have been turned out and had to go and live far enough away so no shame was brought on the family. Now, nobody seemed to get married and that was always called living in sin. And the clothing! You didn't go round showing your bump, you wore loose clothes and were decent about it.

"Well I'm glad I'm not expecting these days." She thought.

But Russ wasn't far from her mind. She'd learnt it was a waste of time to worry over him because it did no good. He was a stubborn lad that always knew best and wouldn't take any advice even if you offered it. But this morning he looked different. She wasn't entirely sure it was a health thing. He'd had a nightmare, that was pretty obvious, but when he used to have them when he was young, there was always a reason behind it. Often she found he was bullied, but other times it was because something was bothering him but he wouldn't say what. But he hadn't had them for years, so there had to be something particular that had caused this. She would mull it over during the day and try and broach the subject gently when he got home that evening.

Rosalie had arrived alone and Lily asked politely where the trainee was hoping the answer would be that she had finished. She wasn't disappointed.

"Oh her. Another waste of time Lily. Didn't last five minutes."

"I thought so. Didn't like her."

As Rosalie was getting the shower ready for her wash she said "I shouldn't say this but I know I can trust you."

"Oh yes?" The ears were up and tuned immediately.

"Well, she was supposed to be a trainee. Ha, trainee my foot. She was a plant I'm telling you. She knew exactly what was supposed to be done and every bit of paper that had to be filled in, and after me she'd be sent onto the next. Well, they must think I fell off the last bus." She almost threw the towel down.

"I didn't trust her, but I knew she was nosing into things."

"You don't miss a trick do you Lily."

All she got in reply was a very wry but knowing smile. Although this elderly lady would remember nothing of the clock or anything that happened, she sensed something had taken place.

"Well when there's nothing better to do, you amuse yourself. I've always liked summing folks up and I wasn't far wrong mostly." Lily seemed to be talking to herself.

Rosalie was just making the usual notes in the record book then putting it back in place she said "I bet you could tell a few tales. What did you do, as a job I mean?"

"Well, you didn't work when you got married, oh no."

"I mean before that." She was picking up a strange sense of something she couldn't place from this lady.

"Oh nothing exciting, you had to take what jobs you could get. There was no messing about, you couldn't pick and choose you had to take what there was."

It was obvious she wasn't going to be any more forthcoming but Rosalie had the strangest feeling she was hiding something.

"Well, I'll see you tomorrow Lily. Your friend coming today?" She couldn't help smiling when she said it.

"I bloody well hope not." Lily wasn't joking.

As she left and got into her car, something was niggling at Rosalie as if it was somewhere in her brain but she couldn't find it. The whole atmosphere had changed in that house since her last visit, even Lily seemed different. Although it sounded absolutely ridiculous, it didn't feel like the same person she had cared for yesterday. This was something she had never experienced. She had been present when old people had died and the relatives had opened the window to let the spirit go free. She never understood that as she had been brought up to believe that soul didn't leave the body for seventy two hours, and of course she tended people from different religious beliefs so had to honour their wishes. But this was different. Glancing in her rear view mirror she saw a familiar figure approaching.

"Oh no. Dracula's mother!"

She started the car and drove off before the woman could get near enough to delay her.

Of course Irene didn't have a key as she had told Russ, although she had often given the impression she was fumbling for one, and rang the bell as usual. She'd seen the carer leave and knew Lily wouldn't hurry herself so she had no option but to wait. After a minute or so she became impatient and started hammering on the door.

"All right, all right, don't bang my frigging door down."

Irene's face was a picture. She stood there, mouth open thinking there must be somebody else in the house.

"I thought it must be you." Lily, as soon as she'd opened the door, turned and walked back to the lounge muttering but loud enough to be heard "You can't have a piss in peace now."

Shocked and amazed Irene followed her into the room and sat down.

"Well, aren't you taking your coat off?" Lily wasn't looking at her.

"I'm not sure if I'm going to stay." The tone was curt.

"What you come for then?"

"I don't think I will even bother to answer that. I don't know what has come over you I don't."

"And there's me, with a tasty bit of tittle tat for you."

"Oh well, I mean I wouldn't want you to.. um ...."

"Miss it. You still want to hear it." Lily finished off for her.

Like Rosalie, Irene knew something was seriously wrong here but what was it? She was trying to work out what was going on so said "Have they altered your medication?"

Irene's guardian was doing her best to pull her away and get her to leave, but Lily had thrown out a carrot which Irene couldn't ignore. If there was gossip, she had to be one of the first to spread it. But that wasn't all. Although she didn't know it yet, Lily was holding her and she could only leave when she released her.

The angels were going frantic and messages were flying to higher sources and although only a few would guess what was happening, those that did knew they had a major problem on their hands which had to be detected and controlled immediately.

Although she would never know how it started, Irene was sitting opposite Lily who was in the middle of a tirade about someone and she made sure the tale would hold this woman transfixed for a considerable time, just long enough for the seeds to be planted.

Russ had felt so ill he had to leave work and go home. But that was the only way the high angels could get him on his own to communicate with him. His mum was still out as he let himself in and he was drawn to go and lie on his bed. For some reason he didn't feel ill now but very bewildered. Something didn't feel right and he knew he had to find out what it was, although somehow he felt he'd rather not know. But that was no option. This was when he would have had Denzil with him and he missed him already. The communication couldn't be made through his guardian as they wouldn't be high enough to be privy to this so another one nearer to Russ's level was detailed to inform and protect him.

The room went very still and quiet and when it was at the right level the high angel came. Russ was relieved to find it was someone familiar to him and Vinn greeted him quickly but indicated there was no time for lengthy conversation.

"There's been an infiltration."

Russ was alert with his senses fully tuned and aware of his normal high position.

"Not at the recall." This was unthinkable.

"Yes but only one. On the ten position."

"That's where my earth mother was positioned."

"It's not her, it's her friend. They replaced her with an evil one and it's now in her physical."

"Lily." Russ said but also needed to know more. "You are sure it's just her?"

"As far as we can ascertain. We checked the others they all seem normal."

The next point was very important.

"Was it a swap or have they taken her body with her still in situ?" Russ had to know.

"She's still there which isn't good but better than.... "He didn't have to elaborate for if she had been removed she could be anywhere and unable to return to her body and may never be traced. That would put her own soul in jeopardy.

"Well at least if we can oust this intruder she may recover sufficiently."

But then the next point had to be addressed. It wasn't why, because the evil was always on the look out to take any souls if the chance was there, it was how? The operation had been so carefully planned and lower levels of spirits were used who would be oblivious to what was happening so couldn't leave thought patterns to be traced. They were basically going about in a semi trance just following instructions fed to them via their instincts. There was always the possibility of a chance sighting as the clock was formed but then they would go for the big fry, the one in the centre spot, but Denzil had departed according to plan.

This left only one possibility which Vinn had to state. There had been an informer.

In earthly matters one would now check computers, cameras, replay videos etc to find the tiny piece of information which would flush out the culprit. It is too complicated to explain the spiritual equivalent but they have much deeper and secret ways of rechecking anything and everything. Within seconds, in our time, they had their answer. It was one of the red dots. Someone who had been monitoring everything from afar and only appeared at the last minute to make sure everything went to plan and the evil was planted. Lisa.

The question most would ask would be, why would she want to place an evil element in Lily? For the simple reason, she is house bound so they could hide there for as long as they needed.

Vinn was still musing as to why they used such an important ritual ie spirit recall just to place an evil entity. Surely they would try to stop the spirit being transported?

"There has to be more to it." Russ said. "They could have planted it now ready for the next recall."

Both of them felt there was a deeper even more threatening reason and it would be their job to find out what it was, quickly.

Russ would have a difficult job from now on. He would have to flit between his high state to communicate with Vinn, then reduce to his earthly level to throw off any scent. But there would always be watchers and they hoped that their own would waylay any unwanted guests.

Irene was getting fed up and rather worried. She had wanted gossip but not her whole brain soaked with stuff which was obvious fiction. What was the matter with her friend? In the end she managed to cut in while Lily was taking a breath.

"I'm sure I don't know what's the matter with you today, but you certainly aren't yourself. And that pack of lies, I suppose that's funny to you, well let me tell you it isn't to me. I'm not sure when I'll come again, if I ever do. So if you're lonely it's your own fault."

With that she put on her coat, grabbed her bag and made her way to the front door. The atmosphere was loaded and she couldn't get out quick enough. As she was going through the doorway she heard a sadistic laugh.

"Oh you will you frumpy old twat."

Irene slammed the door behind her.

"Never."

She was almost in tears as she made her way home. It wasn't so much what Lily had said, but it wasn't right and she didn't know why.

Russ was downstairs when she finally reached her own home and he could see the state she was in.

"Wh..What are you doing home?" She said.

"I felt very ill, but I'm a bit better now. But what's happened to you for goodness sake. You look as though you've seen a ghost."

"I might as well have."

Alarm bells went off. He needed to know more especially in the light of recent news.

"Sit down Mum, I'll make us a cuppa." He helped her off with her coat and put her bag on the table.

After a few minutes, she tried to tell him how she had felt at Lily's and soon became very upset again. He tried to calm her but it had to come out.

"It's as though it wasn't her I'm telling you. If I hadn't seen her, I'd have sworn it was someone else. She was gabbling on and she swore!"

At another time it would have been funny, but Russ was piecing this with the fact that Lisa could have opened the door for the evil to arrive, and this could be it. He summoned Vinn who was there in an instant and thought transferred all this information in a second. This meant that obviously out of the four, Irene wasn't involved, a quick check on Rosalie cleared her, Lily was an innocent receiver and although there was still no proof, Lisa was very much under suspicion at this moment in time.

The higher powers were still checking every participant of the clock but everyone was completely clean which was one blessing at least. Surely high level evil would have taken the opportunity to use this for a mass infiltration, or was this just a dummy run to prove it worked. On those kind of high planes it wouldn't have been very clever, for if they planned to do the same again, the good angels would be waiting for them.

In the state she was in, Irene didn't notice the change in Russ as he communicated his knowledge with Vinn, but it was something he would have to control as she started to come back to her normal self.

Chapter 7

Denzil was now in a totally different state which is not easy to explain in simple terms. You have to take your reasoning beyond the earth, physical awareness, space and even time itself for they play no part in his current and future existence.

We are used to limits, beginnings and endings but in this other place there are none of those. Even if we haven't parented a child we have been aware of family and friends rejoicing in a birth, a new beginning and we have, or will have experienced the death of someone close to us. An ending. But those aware of spirit know that is not the case, for the spirit lives on.

So let us turn our attention to Denzil. By the theory that he had been born seven times and died seven times he was now just existing in spirit. But in space and time there is no beginning or end. So where did he come from in the first place? There was no starting point, he was always there. Now that he had finished his earth time and adjustment time, his spirit was recalled. But he had to be somewhere, because there is no end. If there was a start and finish, what was there before and what will there be afterwards? Maybe astronauts and scientists would understand this better than most, but it is this very difficult for our physical brains to assimilate because we are not used to anything that doesn't bear a time limit. Even the earth is about half way through its life and will cease one day.

Distance is also hard to imagine. We talk about light years but that is still vast. Our galaxy can be up to 200,000 light years across and yet we accept that Denzil was on the other side of the Milky Way, so how far is he now? This is merely to give us a very vague understanding of the extent of the spirit world which one day we will all encounter but it is doubtful if this has even given you the slightest idea of how to understand it.

Denzil did make one correct assumption. Russ couldn't have been the one to be selected because his earth relatives were still living. One can only be recalled when there are none left so you can slip away almost unnoticed.

Obviously a spirit isn't left to wander the universe and beyond, without guidance but for the first moments it is necessary for them to adjust with no interference. Then the group move closer. In this new world you don't have just one guardian angel, you merge into others and combine every scrap of your knowledge and everything you have learnt during your earth lives. So Denzil would never be recognised as himself, for he was now part of a much greater mass more powerful than can be described and it was at this level the most evil entities were attacked and destroyed in the vicinity, but of course they would be despatched to a holding area and then dealt with in a way known only to the highest of powers.

This would also mean that Russ would never encounter his friend again and although he wasn't given the knowledge of the transition, instinct told him he had lost his partner and he had a tremendous sense of bereavement.

With Denzil progressing, there had to be a force to take over where he left off for the evil that had infiltrated had to be disposed of quickly. There was always someone in the wings waiting to step in but they had to be of a very high standing for this kind of evil had a purpose and wouldn't stop until they had achieved their goal. The force that was using Lily at the moment was only one of many in a sadistic group that had no thought for the pain they inflicted but got a buzz from it. Of course they didn't want to use an old woman for anything physical, she was just there for them to use as a hiding place until ready to strike. Something else Lisa had set up for them among many others she had selected while going round the homes of the elderly and vulnerable. She had made sure she was part of the clock and used it as a portal to let the troops in. She wasn't in command, just a dogsbody but the biggest arse sniffer to curry favour with her superiors. If she thought that would earn her brownie points, she was disillusioned for she was merely a tool in their hands. We all know at least one like that. But she thought she had let a few in and would be in charge of them so when she found out that it had been a bigger operation of which she was merely a tiny part, she was angry. Unfortunately, she still had to learn that you didn't retaliate against such evil powers and throwing a strop when things didn't go her way was merely classed as amusing. She was determined to find out the extent of this job and was charging headlong to her downfall, because spirits like that could jeopardise an operation and the higher evil powers wouldn't tolerate that, so she would have to be sorted, permanently.

The good powers have very strict ethics, but sadly the evil do not. If they decided that Lisa would have to be exported for good, that is exactly what they would do. No qualms, no regrets. Anyone who got in their way was, to put it mildly, released from duty, so if a spirit was recalled by evil, it would be a totally different story. Whereas Denzil was about to be part of a fighting force to combat evil, Lisa could be dispensed with in a totally different way. She would still exist, but she would be a lost soul, forever floating aimlessly in a strange place filled with ghastly experiences that no soul should ever have to endure. She wouldn't recognise anyone and the biggest torture would be loneliness. Where? Don't forget, this universe is enormous, and beyond that, infinity.

Chapter 8

Irene was watching Russ as they sat after their evening meal. Neither had felt very hungry but ate so that the other would.

"You've met Lily." She said casually.

"Once, or could have been twice, but when she was able to get about. Haven't seen her for a while though."

"No but you'd recognise her if you saw her again."

Russ realised where this was going and normally would have come out with a choice remark and left the room. But things were different now.

"Oh yes. I mean she hasn't changed all that much I don't suppose." He tried to make it sound as casual as possible.

"Um, you wouldn't do me a favour would you?" She didn't look straight at him.

"Depends. Nothing daft mind." He gave a forced laugh to try and lighten the mood but it didn't seem to work.

"Would I?" She tried to sound shocked. The very thought of it. "Well, I wondered if you'd come with me, oh I know you have to go to work, but say Saturday."

"Suppose I could. What for though?"

"Oh you know, we don't have to stay long. I could say you'd given me a lift. I want you to see if you notice a difference."

Suddenly Vinn sent a warning. Russ could be walking into danger. If the evil that was occupying Lily should recognise him, he could be a target. He hadn't been one of the clock participants but he had certainly been an observer and even this could be a trap.

"You mean they are using mum to get me there?" He sent the thought back.

This was a dilemma. He had no problem with going to see if what his mum was saying was indeed fact, but yes, he could be walking right into danger, maybe not of a high level in the house, but it would be well monitored by higher evil powers.

"I'd like to mum......."

"Oh thank you. That's settled then."

"Mum," he had to say it, "I'm not sure it's a good idea for me or you for that matter to go there at the moment."

Her tone changed.

"I might have known you'd make excuses. I don't ask much but......"

It was his turn to cut her off.

"Mum. It may not be safe."

"Safe? What do you mean safe? What are you talking about?"

Now he had put himself in an awkward position. Vinn came to the rescue with a thought. Yes, he could use that.

"Mum, I don't like to tell you this but there's been some bug going round at work, not a nice one and I may have had a mild version of it, that's why I had to come home today. Also they don't want me back tomorrow, or until I'm sure it's gone. I'm just hoping I haven't passed it on to you."

"Oh I see." Then thought "So that's why he looked a bit peaky this morning.". "Well in that case, I think you are wise. We will go when you feel better."

That didn't exactly solve the problem but it would buy some time and hopefully the evil would have left Lily in the meantime. He sent a 'thank you' to Vinn along with a sigh of relief.

They made polite conversation, watched a bit of television then as soon as he could Russ said he would like to go to bed.

"Good idea, I won't be too long myself." Irene agreed. "Is there anything we should be taking for this bug?"

"Just plenty of rest Mum. It will run its course."

"Oh alright. I'll probably just ring your aunt Vi and warn her it's going around."

"Oh she'll love that!" He thought to himself but just nodded in reply and went upstairs.

Immediately he was safely in his room Vinn was ready to give him the latest update but started with "Good bit of teamwork there."

"You got me out of a hole." Russ agreed.

"We think we've identified the one who's camping in Lily."

"Oh yes?"

"Going back a bit but there was a very nasty session started in South America several years back and it gradually seemed to be creeping over the earth on the larger land masses. It never got to the smaller islands because we obliterated it."

"Oh that was a horrible evil, it worked on people's minds until hatred ruled and they were virtually killing each other, in the most terrible ways."

"And thriving on it."

Russ hoped this wasn't going where he thought.

"Tell me it's not the same one again."

"Not exactly. This one is not physical which makes it harder to recognise. But it is just as lethal. It attacks the mind, so people go mad. They don't kill each other, they kill themselves because they can't bear the effects."

There was complete stillness for a moment.

"But why now?"

Russ was still grieving for Denzil and secretly wished he was here, no disrespect to Vinn but he still felt he had lost his twin where they thought alike, acted alike and didn't have to even exchange a suggestion as the other had already got it.

Vinn knew what he was going through and offered "He could still be helping you know."

"How? Don't even know where he is by now."

So that mind patterns couldn't be intercepted each put him from their thinking.

Little did either of them realise just how much he would be involved in what was to come.

This is another example of how different things are in the spirit world. For example, if someone has lost a relative or dear friend, it is very comforting to feel that they are near, especially in times of illness or sorrow, and yes, you can feel the presence and although it may be a shock to learn that they aren't actually at your side, with the power of the protection they use, they might just as well be. This may raise a question. It is understandable that if the spirit has relatives still on earth, they are likely to be near but when the spirit is recalled, they are supposed to have gone for good, or at least to a place too far away to be in contact.

It is like many things that are general belief, we can surmise but we won't actually know until it is our turn. But think again. Couldn't the information be fed to us if there seemed to be no other way of combatting the evil forces, especially the higher ones? Although when a spirit is recalled and they can no longer return to earth, which is but is a tiny area, they will still be existing somewhere and we know how vast space is.

It is therefore important to view things from this aspect at this point or it may be confusing if Denzil may appear to be guiding certain happenings.

When people have taken part in a clock formation, some are never used again for various reasons, but some can be regulars and as soon as one departure has settled, they are lined up for the next one. In a way it is as though they are living two existences. They go about their daily lives as they have always done, then they have the clock duty running parallel. The physical and the spiritual are normal, but in a way there are three existences because their own spirit carries on almost oblivious of how they are being used because the forces cloak it from their knowledge. When this is being operated by good angels there is no problem but some are totally under the control of evil. Imaging a complete clock with all participants ruled by evil and not to recall the spirits, but to place them, in other words a complete reverse of the recent procedure. The fact that an evil entity had infiltrated when Denzil was transported gave rise to very high level concern because it had appeared to be too easy.

Lisa was under close scrutiny but she had none of the usual vibrations that were associated with evil infiltration, so it could be thought that she was just being used to draw the attention to her while the main operation was going on unobserved. This was an old trick but could not be overlooked. It was also possible that she hadn't actually brought the evil in, but merely been in presence.

The high evil use innocent people all the time which is why, as soon as the operation, whatever it is at the time, is completed they leave them to be watched but they are nothing more than a decoy and the person themselves can be completely unaware of it.

"So this Lisa may be a dead end." Vinn had been observing her going about her job with no apparent guards attached and they could be wasting valuable time.

"But I want to know what is using Lily." Russ knew this had to be more than a distraction. He had felt a slight residue on his mother when he was near her and it was usually a sign when something was lingering and that it was active.

Then it hit them both and Vinn voiced it.

"It's been brought here!"

They took stock of it for a moment. Lisa, whether a tool or not, had left a deposit on Lily and that had been transferred in a minor way to Irene who had now passed it on to Russ. On recap, it had been accidentally/on purpose supposed that Russ was going for recall, to hide the fact of it being Denzil. When that mucked up any plans, the enemy must have targeted Russ in his human form.

"But why would you have been selected in the first place?" Vinn was feeling that something was eluding him. "You are still earth bound by Irene and Vi."

There was a distinct pause before Russ replied.

"I'm not actually."

"What?"

"Irene is not my mother. I was born out of wedlock and put up for adoption. And before you ask, both my natural parents have passed over, and of course Aunt Vi is also not a blood relative."

"Bloody hell!" Vinn would have been open mouthed had he been in body, but was trying to get everything in its right place. "So you have no living relatives?"

"None whatsoever."

"And you knew this all along. So why in damnation's name didn't you say?"

Russ knew how this must sound and had to think carefully before he tried to make it sound plausible.

"Well, you see Denzil and I are soul mates. Have been for as long as I know, but when each of us have been in body, much of our knowledge is screened from us. We got odd memories but it was never anything conclusive. But it was always understood that as we arrived together if you like, we would both be recalled together."

"So that was one hell of a shock when he went and you didn't."

"I felt ripped apart. He is my other half, we operate together. When we said we were twins we didn't just use it as a fancy name, it meant we were part of each other and I cannot function without him."

"No wonder you look ill." Vinn was at a loss for how to comfort him but he knew nothing would, not until they were reunited. "So where do we go from here?"

Russ tried to be practical and look at the whole picture to get some sense out of it.

"Well there's two things as far as I can make out."

"And the first is. Let me guess." Vinn had an idea. "Perhaps only one of you could go at a time. It could have been you or Denzil. Have you ever known of more than one to go through a clock system?"

There was a pause,

"I wouldn't know." Russ grabbed this like a lifeline but then said "And what's your second idea?"

"You know what it is. Perhaps you should have gone anyway, either alone or together, but the evil was trying to split you, so it may not have mattered which of you went as long as they got one, and as you are the one in body….."

"They kept me." Russ was still thinking. "You know what I don't understand, when Denzil was just starting to be lifted he was sending out the message that I couldn't have gone anyway because I had earthly connections. But he knew the truth so why would he do that?"

Together they chorused "To hide the true fact." Russ finished it off saying "and so they could keep me here?"

Vinn was triumphant.

"They had to split you up. For some reason you were too much of a danger together." But then he added "But which one?"

"I don't follow you."

"Why not keep Denzil?"

Russ thought and then answered "Maybe because I am in body and what they want to use me for, or whatever their plan is, one of us still had to be."

After a moment Vinn said "You are too involved. I'm stepping back looking at it from the outside."

"And what do you see?" Russ wasn't expecting anything mind blowing.

"I think it's ok if one of you is on earth and the other in total spirit, but they can't have you both working completely on the same plane. So as you are here, you had to stay here."

"Well I suppose it makes sense when you put it that way. But it must be something pretty important to go to those lengths. I mean there's unlimited levels above us, high as we may be, so what is it that is in their pipeline?"

"I'm sorry to say but that is something we have yet to find out."

Although he may have been light years away, Denzil was privy to this conversation and was glad Russ had shared the truth for it was obvious that it was no secret among the evil powers. The question that he also pondered was why? But he would stay in constant touch in his own way which cannot be described in physical terms.

Violet was getting ready to go out. It had warmed up a bit but she still took a jacket as it could be a bit cooler when she came home but at least she had the light nights. She met up with Janet as usual and together they made their way to the vicarage, were greeted by Sam and followed the vicar into the conservatory. They never queried why a gardener worked strange hours and was always there when they visited.

Denzil was observing the clock formations very closely. They seemed to be a bit what he called untidy. Normally, the participants, that is the blue dots would meet to build up their position. It didn't have to be simultaneous as long as all the positions were primed. For example Vi and Janet went in the evening and Irene would go to Lily in the daytime but this was no accident. On one clock there were of course twelve positions but there was a ring of them round towns and cities so it would draw too much attention to have everyone making a pilgrimage at a certain time each day. As long as all were covered, the power needed was there. But it wasn't happening this time. Some clock positions hadn't had anyone check in at all whereas others were almost ready. It seemed like nobody was in overall control but then he realised what was happening. It wasn't getting ready for a recall. It was prepared for an invasion but was it from the high angels or the opposite? Pure evil.

Although Denzil was still connected to this particular area there was a good reason for it. Many things had churned through his thoughts since the transition. At first he seemed to be alone but that was for him to readjust to his new state which is very different to someone who is between lives or very spiritually aware whilst still in body. It is true, on total recall there is no going back, but he wasn't complete and he felt he couldn't move on completely until Russ had joined him. Fortunately, he was on his last earth life so when that was complete, he too should be on total recall.

One point of explanation. If someone is called from body temporarily they are on recall, but when they will no longer be returning to the physical plane, they are on total recall.

Denzil wasn't sure just how long he had been in this state until it was explained by one of his mentors.

"You now do not exist in time or space, so don't try and use those factors. You are trying to think of how many earth hours or days since you were called, but that is not in the equation. Also don't try to work out how far you are from the earth for there are no miles, or measurements to work with. It matters little where you are, the fact remains that you can still observe and even adjust or manipulate happenings without having to be anywhere near."

He thought for a moment.

"But if I want to influence Russ, wouldn't it have to be when he could receive?"

His guide was amused but this was normal for recent arrivals.

"Let me ask you. When you were in body, how many times did you get a sudden inspiration or thought? When you were asleep, did you wake suddenly with something going round in your brain?"

"Of course! Why didn't I realise that?" Denzil felt silly at not haven't worked that out for himself having been in spirit for so long but when one is adjusting to new surroundings or places and even situations, logical thought can get a bit confused.

He was far from the earth, yet it was as if he was still there. This he was informed was a usual practice for safety as it took much longer for evil to track a source by which time it had been moved.

"But doesn't that also work in reverse? Wouldn't evil do the same?" He asked.

"Of course. But there are different ways of doing things."

Denzil knew he wasn't going to learn any more at this stage so turned his attention back to Russ. If only he knew when he would be able to join him but that would mean an early earth death. For now he would have to be content with just being able to contact him on a regular basis.

His guide cut into his thoughts.

"Don't plan on those lines. You have other demands on your work."

It was hard adjusting to this new experience. Up to now he'd been used to working in spirit and basically going where and when he liked, but this was different. It reminded him of when you went to a new school, or moved up in class and it was almost like starting again. He was a fairly high level angel and yet now he felt like the new boy. So who was above him and to what levels? If that was anything like time and space he would have a long wait to find out, if he ever did.

"There is movement in the clocks."

The message came as an order, in other words, stop musing and start working.

"Well slap my wrists." Went through his mind as he projected to the clocks around Riverbank. Still there seemed no pattern to it. But then as more arrived he could see. It was only the four main compass points that were being manned, plus the stabilisers so the vicar would need to be present, which he was, and Lily's group wouldn't be required this time. But then he noticed something different. Lisa, who was at ten o'clock before was now the red dot at nine. He immediately checked twelve and three position but they were still empty.

His spiritual thoughts were still on his earth connections and there were two main factors to which he needed answers. But he didn't even have to ask the questions before he instinctively knew.

Number one. Accepting that Irene was not Russ's earth mother, wouldn't there still be a connection because she had legally adopted him and brought him up, so there would be a tie preventing him from recall. The answer was rather harsh he felt. If there is a strong bond, yes it would hold a spirit to the adoptive parent but in this case, there is no bond. He is free to be moved. That provoked mixed emotions. Firstly, Russ would be free to join him, but when there is no bond it can cause problems for the other soul may not be a good element and can prevent a free transition. In other words, Irene could have been simply monitoring him for evil forces waiting to claim him for their own use whenever they wished.

Number two. What about the other one? Although it was not a subject he was ever supposed to discuss, he had to ask. The answer was immediate.

"There are two of you."

It was always the same. He knew there had been three of them originally and suddenly the third one had been snatched and disappeared as if he had never existed. He seemed to remember he had only been with them for one earth life but after that it was as though he had never existed. Even Russ seemed loathe to answer, so it always made Denzil think he must know about it but he was like a closed book. Surely this was the time to be told the truth. Well, maybe now he would have more power to do just that. It did explain why he was always obsessed with the number three and why everything must always divide or result in three. Whether it was against the wishes, or orders of his elders, he would make it his project to get to the bottom of it.

Of course his thoughts were being monitored which sent a wave of caution through many levels. He must be prevented at all costs from learning the truth so a shield was put in place to contain it. If he should bypass or get through it, the consequences could prove fatal, not only to mankind but to the entire spectrum of good powers anywhere in the vastness of space.

Sam was carefully monitoring the movements at the vicarage. He had to make sure that it was always the same two who came to meet the vicar's wife. He was well tuned in this area and knew that if somebody new arrived it could be for a very good reason. Although some controllers were moved around, he always insisted on remaining in the same place and this wasn't queried, for sometimes a spirit could be, for the want of a better description, under cover. Of course they were well vetted. You couldn't just let anyone say I want to do this or be here, but there were ways of knowing if someone was genuine.

Although he had been involved in centuries of this kind of operation, he never took anything for granted, and without anyone's knowledge always studied the full background of subjects he was working with. Violet and Janet were no problem. They lived this and past lives quite simply without a lot of ambition and were perfect tools as they drew little or no attention to themselves. They didn't even know what part they played as they only remembered what they were allowed.

But he was not comfortable with either the vicar or his wife. As he was being used as a stabiliser, the vicar would have to be fairly competent and experienced yet there was something that didn't sit right with Sam. He had tried all ways to find out but it was as though he wasn't supposed to know and that always aroused his curiosity. The man's wife was not the person one would place in that role. She was not outgoing, barely spoke when she went to church, and never took part in any social activities whereas most are very involved. It was as though everything went on around her and she was oblivious to it. There was nothing else for it. He was going to have to make a move.

His guardian was on high alert. This was something Sam shouldn't be doing, but knowing his experience, if something was affecting him that strongly there had to be a reason for it and he needed all the protection possible, but covertly.

The three ladies were in the conservatory. Although they couldn't be seen from the road or the church they were still on full view to Sam and made no attempt to block his view, as if they were all fully aware of his red dot position. So now they sat in their usual formation in complete silence. Knowing they wouldn't be stirring for a while, Sam carefully made his way to the side of the house which wasn't overlooked. He passed the kitchen window and slowed almost to a stop. The next window was the side one of the lounge and it was possible the vicar would be there. Very slowly he crept nearer until he could see in, but he wasn't prepared for the sight that would greet him. The vicar was on his kneels, his hands together in prayer and he was looking up, tears streaming down his face. His lips were moving but Sam wasn't in a good enough position to lip read. But Sam's guardian was picking up every syllable and relaying it to the higher powers. The vicar was begging for forgiveness and asking to be released from this terrible position he was now in. It seems he had been selected as a stabiliser when spirits were recalled, but that was by the good angels. Recently something hadn't felt right and the alert had shot through all levels that the evil archangels were infiltrating the clock formations and seizing innocent souls for their own purpose, which meant the ones on total recall would never reach their ultimate existence.

No one was expecting the next move. All clocks were terminated.

Vi and Janet looked at each other then at the vicar's wife wondering just what they were doing. Janet broke the ice.
"Well it was lovely to see you. Thank you for having us."
And the two friends made their exit as quickly as they could. The vicar's wife was completely bewildered but before she could ask her husband what was going on, he was at the door bidding the two 'goodbye' as though it was an everyday thing. But he was different. The strain had gone and he knew his prayers had been answered, for now anyway.
"Did you invite them?" His wife asked very curtly when they were back in the lounge.
"They've been before." Was all he would offer.
He was waiting for her to ask more questions but they didn't come and she went back into her quiet mode.
"I think I need a cup of tea." He said moving towards the kettle. He didn't expect a reply and she had already gone into the lounge but he sensed a strong feeling of defeat.

"Now why would she feel that?" He thought but was just happy to think he may have thrown a spanner in the works for now. Well someone had been listening, of that he was certain.

Sam had a strange feeling. Couldn't be coincidence could it, that after seeing the vicar as he had, then the women leaving, then the clock was obliterated? But a strange sense of peace came over him even if it was going to be temporary.

"Ah well, there'll be no more meetings in the glasshouse." He thought as he tidied up his tools.

Spirits in human form for a specific purpose like Sam, were invaluable tools of information and communication. They went about their daily business hardly noticed which was what made them so effective. Now he would waiting for his next instructions but he knew that something would have to be put in place for despatching the recalls. It could only stay on hold for so long.

"Well somebody better get ready for the backlog." He laughed as he cast a look at the vicarage when he left for home.

Chapter 9

Friday was going to be a very demanding day in all areas. Russ was not going to work as physically he didn't feel at all well and mentally he was in torment and couldn't think straight. Irene was beginning to drive him mad saying that if he wasn't fit to go to work he should see the doctor. He just needed time to adjust but how could he explain that to her?

"Well I think its your hormones again."

She often came out with that when she didn't know what else to blame but she never actually looked at him when she said it.

"If you so much as mention those f…"

"I hope you weren't going to use filthy words in this house my lad. You know my feelings on that subject."

"Only too well." He spoke instead of just thinking his reply this time.

"Well don't forget we said we'd go and see Lily tomorrow. So you'd better buck your ideas up."

He began to wish he'd forced himself to go to work after all, but he hadn't got the strength. It was as though all the life blood had been drained from his body. As he sat or rather flopped in the chair, something shot into his head as though he had been given a message.

"Three!"

Instantly he was alert now. That could have only come from one source. Denzil.

"I need to go and lie down."

He wasn't asking, he was telling his mother and he'd gone before she could even open her mouth to reply. He lay on his bed, eyes closed and opened his mind to receive.

Again "Three."

He remembered how his twin was always making figures come back to three in some way.

"What are you trying to tell me?" He sent.

After a moment a very faint "Find three." Wafted over him. It was strange, it wasn't like any verbal message, or even one from spirit. It was almost like a desperate plea. Also the strange thing was that, although so quiet it felt as though it had been cut off, terminated as though he wasn't supposed to hear it and it was going from his mind so he had to concentrate to keep it there but whatever it was, was stronger and within seconds he had forgotten the word. It had been spiritually wiped so that he mustn't even think it.

This was cause for concern in high places. Denzil had been warned to let it go but obviously he was desperately trying to contact Russ for him to find the third. If he didn't stop, it would jeopardise his eventual fate. Only top notch spirits rise to the very high levels, and although Denzil was qualified, if he insisted on disobeying this rule he would never achieve it. There had to be a close watch on him at all times for he would try anything to find his number three, no matter what it cost.

He was being moved great distances to try and shake him out of this obsession and it was early days, so there was still time. He was a brilliant operator but he still had to step up to the mark.

In other realms, there was great discussion about the clocks. They knew that it had to be sorted quickly but safely and it may mean changing the recall route although it would have to be just as, if not more secure than previously. Quite unexpectedly Denzil let it be known that he had a plan. Some angels were all for dismissing it before he had put it forward, but others always kept open thoughts and wanted to know more.

"You do realise he expects a bargain don't you?" One objector stated. "We get his absolutely mind blowing plan, but he wants information."

Unfortunately, some had to agree but still wanted to know what he had to offer.

"Why don't we feed him false facts?" Was one suggestion but was squashed immediately.

"He's not that stupid. He is ultra clever and would see though it, especially if it was too easy."

"Well then, keep him on a promise. Say we will tell him what he wants, when we have the plan of course."

"You are not dealing with a school boy here. In some cases he is way better than us. He's certainly no fool."

After a moment one angel said "We don't even know if he has got the answer to it, do we?"

They were all deep in thought for a time because this was a difficult choice and they didn't realise that, even from a great distance, he was monitoring their conversation. Yes, he did have a plan, and as they expected it would cost them and all he wanted was to know was one simple thing. Who and where is three?

Lily, or rather the entity that was using her bodily form at the moment, was getting restless. Something must have gone wrong. This Rosy person wasn't whom she had been led to believe was there to help in this part of the operation. Of course the spirit didn't have to be male or female but took on the identity of the host, so would be referred to as she.

"Why do they always send you? Haven't they got anybody else. I'm sick of the same face every day." Was the greeting Rosalie got when she did her Friday visit.

This spirit was not operating well. Anyone would know that Rosalie knew Lily like the back of her hand and would notice a sudden change in her temperament. Of course people did change with dementia and such conditions, but this was just a bit too sudden to be real. Fortunately she had come into contact with such situations before so was playing it very carefully. At first she had thought Irene needed careful watching, although nobody would have ever guessed for she went about her daily visits as though that was all she was aware of. But she didn't miss the slightest thing.

She had to hide her thoughts when Lisa had arrived as she knew this person would pick up on anything. From the start she didn't like her. It was one of those times when you can't say exactly why, but something doesn't sit right. The hardest moment was when they were in clock formation and she had sensed a horrible feeling of being used although she couldn't explain it. That was what was eating at her. She always needed to know why because there had to be a reason, and she had learned the hard way to always follow your instincts even if they sound silly at the time.

As this can put a good soul in danger, extra support was brought in to hover in the background and act if necessary.

"Is your friend coming today?" Rosalie tried to sound casual.

"What?"

"I asked if your friend was coming to visit you." She spoke slowly and very distinctly.

"Will you stop treating me like an idiot. I'm not deaf and I'm not stupid, so stop being so bloody patronising."

Rosalie looked at her and said "Well I think there is only one thing I can suggest."

"Oh yes, miss clever clogs, and what's that when it's at home?"

"Well I am going to pass you to the mental health team. So you will be seeing even more strange faces."

"What the bloody hell are you talking about. I'm not senile you know. I know what's what."

Now Rosalie was ready for the punchline.

"I'd better inform your daughter."

"What? I mean… daughter?"

"Yes Lily your daughter. Obviously she will have to be in on this."

"I…I.. what for? What's it got to do with her?"

"Who?"

The evil didn't like this as it knew she was playing with it.

"Look just piss off. You've done what you came to do."

Rosalie smiled.

"Bye Lucy. I hope you like the one that comes tomorrow."

There was no reply for a moment.

"Well why aren't you coming?" Was called as she got to the door.

"Oh I'll be back. To see Lily." Was the parting shot with the emphasis on the name.

The evil watchers knew they had to do something with this carer woman for they weren't sure just how high a level she was and hadn't been fooled for a minute. The good forces on the other hand, were concerned that she had gone in without sufficient protection because she wouldn't be aware of the back up which was in place, and as far as she knew it was a personal fight.

But the homework had already been done. Lisa had been there for long enough to carry out a spiritual scan, and she knew this good person's weaknesses. She reckoned she didn't need help but could deal with her on her own.

This was a common fault. The target may be a push over, but there were always those of a much stronger calibre waiting to do the job properly.

The one question of course was 'where was Lily?' There can be two situations. One where the evil takes over the body and removes its proper occupant, or it can cohabit. If the latter was true, poor Lily would be going through a mental torment. The thing wasn't just coming and going, it was there all the time. One of Rosalie's guardians was given the task and when it was found that Lily was still there, they put her spirit into the equivalent of suspended animation, so she would feel no discomfort and remember nothing when the evil had left.

Denzil and Russ had been informed of this and so it was important to stop Irene going to visit. The less people in the house the better so the evil could be studied without distraction.

Russ went downstairs.

"Oh are you feeling better? I was thinking I must take Lily some cake. She likes my cake."

"Mum." Russ tried to break into the flow.

"I wonder if there's anything else she needs."

"Mum. Please listen. I'm not well enough and I don't think you should go either."

"Well it doesn't have to stop me going. She's probably lonely."

"Mum. You could pass something on, and then if she got it and died...."

"Russell! What are you saying? That's being over protective, or whatever it is"

It was obvious that she wasn't going to back down, but they couldn't let her walk into the house with the evil presence there. Denzil sent the thought to leave it and it would be sorted in other ways. Russ wasn't totally reassured by that as he was only too well aware of what 'other ways' could mean but he had no choice.

It wasn't only the evil presence that had to be contained, but the fact that Lisa was involved and could even be in charge of what was going on at the house, although that did seem highly unlikely. She was more of the willing to please her master kind, but could also be dispensed with at their pleasure.

Although up to this point Denzil may seem to have been a free soul, projecting where he wished, it was quite the opposite. It takes a long time to adjust to a new surrounding and especially existing in a different state. People often think that when they pass on, they will then know everything but it is then they start to realise just how little it is. Nobody wanders about aimlessly. On a normal transition there are helpers waiting to make it as smooth as possible but if you die from any form of trauma, a specialist team takes over.

Total recall goes much further. Although Denzil didn't realise, there was an army of protectors to take him from the clock portal and his tutors had never left him but they had to give him time to readjust. Previously when his soul passed over, he knew he would be returning at some point, but not now. He could never occupy a body in any form and had to exist in total spirit for ever. But since he had been shown how little the earth was in the overall pattern of things, he began to realise how much attention people in body pay situations that are not that important.

What was the most difficult to take in was that he had been round most of the solar system and way beyond already but could still communicate with Russ and anyone else he chose. He was constantly reminded of the fact that time and distance only existed in earth terms and that nowhere else the length of a day would be the same.

But now he was very much concentrating on Russ and his mother and also the evil at Lily's. There was something else. He had noticed Lisa a few times and something was bugging him. He must have met her in a previous life as she seemed very familiar but not as she looked now. There was a distinct difference about her and he traced back to see if he could place her.

Russ knew he was around which gave him a lot of comfort but was told in no uncertain terms to stay put and not follow him as it could be very dangerous at the moment. Reluctantly he obeyed as he knew it had to but he was on the alert the whole time hoping he would get a running commentary.

"Just rest tonight. Nothing will happen." Denzil's words were an instruction not a request.

Sleep was the last thing on Russ's mind but somehow he was starting to get very drowsy and was soon snoring peacefully. But Denzil had already arranged what his dreams would be, so that his twin couldn't follow him.

He was soon observing Lily's house and saw immediately what was resident in her body. It was one of those entities that he called free lance. They would work for, and with anyone as long as it suited their purpose. They would never be leaders, they hadn't got the talent and preferred to leave it to others to do the worrying. Both had met a few like that on earth. This one was having a field day being as annoying as it possibly could and was happy to stay in situ for as long as it was needed, then it would clear off and annoy the hell out of somebody else. At least it was no actual threat although it was an evil sprite, but it was just being used for the purpose of its current employer. Denzil could have removed it in a flash if he wished but it was only the bait and best left well alone. He'd seen them used to draw spirits out into the open to be picked off by high evil, then told to disappear, so was that what was going on here? It must have been placed for a reason. The idea did come to him that it was being used by good angels to flush an evil out. This was why it was dangerous to go in half cocked because you could be working against your own side.

"Well it's not going anywhere." He decided, so he needn't waste time here. But still Lisa was niggling at him but he wondered if he should leave her for a while just in case he was jeopardising another operation. But at the back of his thoughts sat the same thing. Three.

Because Irene had made up her mind, she had to go and see Lily, nothing would stop her and Russ's advice only made her more determined. The strange thing was she didn't feel comfortable going alone now and wanted her son with her for support. Some people would have stayed away after the previous reception but something was forcing her to go. She had tried to sound as if everything was alright by suggesting the cakes, but it wasn't from any benevolent reason. She felt she didn't have to take that load of verbal any more, yet her curiosity forced her to find out just what was going on. If she was honest, this was the juiciest bit she'd had for a long time and just wait until she started spreading it around.

She knew how Russ felt and so slipped out of the house before he was up. He wouldn't be about yet if he wasn't feeling well so there would be no explanations needed. As she got nearer to Lily's house, her pace was slowing and a heavy sensation was in her stomach. At one point she was tempted to turn round and go back but as it wasn't far now the thought of a sit down was more appealing.

She recognised the car outside as the one used by the carer and thought it was a bit early for her visit, so a feeling of dread crept in as she wondered if anything had happened. As she got to the front door her hand froze before she could knock or ring the bell and it was as if she was being pulled away but she had come this far and anyway she wanted to be the first to know if anything was amiss.

The decision was made for her as Rosalie was just coming out.

"Oh, hello Irene. Just give us a minute will you. Got to get something from the car. You can sit in it if you like. Take the weight off."

The suggestion certainly sounded better than standing at the doorway.

"That's kind of you. Anything the matter?"

"No, don't you concern yourself. I won't be long." After making sure Irene was safely in the car she returned to the house.

"Well, that was a load of eyewash if ever I heard it."

She thought but was secretly glad she would be the first to know once she got inside. The need to be the spreader of 'information' as she liked to call it was never far from her mind and this was probably going to be a good one. She sat there wondering for what seemed to be an age but then Rosalie came out and said "You can see her, but I wouldn't stay too long if I were you."

"What's the matter then?"

"Oh she's had a bit of a funny turn but the doctor's been and given her a sedative so don't tire her will you?"

Irene had no option but to follow her into the house and immediately she could feel the difference but as soon as she entered the room, the sight that met her made her shudder. This couldn't be the same person. Lily lay propped up in bed and although she was on medication, something didn't feel right. The aggression had gone but it still didn't have Lily's feel to the place. It was completely empty.

She moved to the bed and put her hand on Lily's. There was no response.

"Hello Lily. It's me, Irene. How are you?"

The eyes were closed and the mouth slightly opened but no words came.

"Is she......?" Irene couldn't bring herself to say it.

Rosalie spoke quietly.

"Not yet, but it won't be long. A nurse from one of the care foundations is arriving soon. I'm just waiting till they come."

"Is it alright if I hold her hand?"

"Of course. She will know although you won't notice any response. I'll let you have a few minutes alone." And she left the room.

The next few moments were very emotional as Irene said how sorry she was the way she had felt and things she'd said because Lily wasn't herself and was obviously ill. She couldn't bear to say dying. She knew now this was why she had known she had been willed to come today.

Unfortunately, it had been the evil powers that had brought her, much against the intervention of the good ones. They had to get their 'plant' to Russ somehow, and as he hadn't come, it had to be through her. The longer she was there the stronger it would be. The original 'free lancer' had been dispensed with as they were no longer needed but had kept the place open ready for the true evil to occupy.

Irene couldn't feel this new interloper as it was very adept in hiding its presence, but she would soon be aware of the effects as it transferred itself from her to Russ, then she, having fulfilled her use would easily be dispensed with.

If only people could see how they are being used without their knowledge.

Immediately a strong protective wall was put round Russ and it didn't matter who knew but it was hoped it had been positioned in time. Denzil was well aware of this operation and added his own protection.

Russ woke up and wondered what time it was, what day, and felt there was something he should be doing. He rubbed his eyes. Almost midday!

"That's strange. Wonder why mum hasn't pestered me by now." He said to himself, then almost immediately "Three."

He put on enough to look decent and went downstairs.

"Where is she?"

He had just decided she must have popped out for a bit of shopping when it came to him.

"Oh she's gone to that friend of hers."

But then another thought registered.

"Oh bloody hell. I'm in for a load of verbal when she gets back."

Realising that she had wanted him to take her and he'd refused, she'd gone anyway. As if something prodded his memory as he made a drink, he remembered what she had said about something not feeling right and an alarm bell started ringing.

"I should have gone." He thought but immediately a message was put into his brain that he had done the right thing but that she should also have kept away. He was on full alert now and somehow his strength had returned and he felt pretty well back to normal. He reached for his mobile and went to call her but then he remembered that she hadn't always got hers, in fact she had never got it with her. He'd bought it for her saying she would be safe as she could always reach him and also if she had a problem like getting home or something. But she said she could never master the thing and the buttons were too small and she couldn't see it properly etc. etc. The truth was she was afraid of it. He looked round the room, and there it was.

The other option was to ring her friend, but that would sound as if he was checking on her. He didn't know the surname and had to think of the Christian name. But something was still not sitting right. Vinn was trying to urge him to stay put and build up his protection for when she got home. He was safe while he was alone, for she would have to actually transfer the evil to him.

Here was a dilemma. The evil knew that as soon as Irene had transferred the physical evil, they would terminate her because that's how callous they were. You've done your job. Goodbye. Some were kept for other purposes but they were evil based and thrived on the work. Irene's sort were always a problem because they thought too much instead of getting on with it.

From the angel's side, there was only one alternative. If she was going to be disposed of anyway, then it must be done before she had the chance to pass the evil. One angel raised a question.

"But the evil will still exist, so won't she have been ended for nothing?"

"But it mustn't reach Russ. Harsh as that sounds."

An elder intervened.

"It can be destroyed at the point of leaving her. There is a way, but we have to bring in the 'others'. This was a term only used when absolutely necessary and never referred to at any other time.

"Can you do it?" One asked as only certain hierarchy had the knowledge.

The only reply was "It can be done."

A very quick decision was made and agreed by all present.

Denzil had homed in on all of this and knew that although it would be a shock to Russ's physical state, he would understand the reasoning behind it. The evil being used was stronger each time, so if this one had been allowed to take root, it would pave the way for a greater force coming in. It had to have a connection to the clocks and the recalls.

His attention turned again to Lisa who seemed to have left the scene as though she had been dismissed but that wasn't how she worked. She was about somewhere probably observing everything and must have had a hand in the Lily situation. He mused on the roundabout way the evil seemed to be working but that wasn't a new thing. Lisa was a red dot and was connected with the blues at ten o'clock one minute then changed position. After she had been to Lily's in body, Lily was possessed, then the evil was supposed to be transferred through Irene to Russ. If she was at the root of it, why not just transfer to him, she had the opportunity, or would that be too obvious. It depended on who was actually pulling her strings.

Then a new thought flowed through him. Was Russ a decoy or a means to an end? There was so much attention building on him, but where was his actual spirit leaning most of the time. That put a different light on things. He, Denzil was the objective. He was mulling it over in a different light now. If they were trying to take him on his recall, the angels knew and that was why Russ was put in the limelight as the one to be lifted knowing all the time that it would be him would be raised.

This was a lot more serious. As final recall is what it says, final, you are out of the way of many levels of attack. It can only be ones of extreme power that can be of any threat and then you are protected by those around you to a maximum degree. But if you are prevented from that transition, you will never achieve the ultimate levels. It had been tried many times in order to prevent the high angels from taking their place but usually without success. If this should be the case now, the evil must consider him a serious threat or they wouldn't go to these lengths.

He was still intrigued to know just which bit was masterminding this. The next thing that invaded his summing up was one word. Three.

The hierarchy were concerned at the fact that this was becoming an obsession and would hamper his ultimate position. There had to be some way to get him to leave it alone. They knew he wouldn't fall for any tricks regarding false information and unfortunately, he seemed bent on making this his prime task.

"He won't give up until he knows." One said.
"Then it is his choice, unless...."
The angels in conference waited wondering what could possibly be the answer?
"We give him one." There was instant consternation and thoughts of "Impossible" and "We can't do that."
Although it sounded a bit far fetched, and was a possibility, there was one major flaw, in fact there were two. In the first place he probably wouldn't fall for it, especially if it was made too easy and the second would be worse. He could become so attached thinking the trio was complete, but what about Russ? He may not accept a third. He loved Denzil and was used to there only being two of them. One spirit also suggested that Denzil would instinctively know it wasn't the right one. All these were valid points and so, for the time being the subject was dropped from discussion but observations would still be on full power.

Russ was getting anxious. It was after two o'clock and his mum still wasn't home. Then the phone rang and made him jump.
"Hello."
"Hello Russ, it's Mum." She was crying. "Lily's just died. I was holding her hand. I didn't know she was ill, I thought she was just being nasty. I feel so ashamed, and me being a church goer and all."
A shock wave ran through him. Instinct told him there was more to it than this but he kept his voice calm.
"Calm down Mum. It's alright I'm here. She is at peace now."
"I know." She sobbed. "I've got to go because the doctor is coming to... you know... say that its right."
"Yes I know Mum. I'll come a fetch you. Try and stay calm." As soon as he'd said it, he knew it was she wouldn't.
Denzil was panicking. Russ couldn't go because if something happened to her, it could happen to him as well, and this wasn't how it was supposed to be.
Irene was about to put the phone down then made him promise that he would be there as soon as he could.

Even the high angels were alert now. Was this all planned? But something wasn't right. If she was supposed to transfer the evil to him in body, he could not be terminated as well. Things were changing quickly and they had to stay ahead of the game.

The attention was soon on Lily's house with all the comings and goings. It doesn't take long for people to realise something has happened and soon a little group had formed.

"Has she had a fall? I've not seen an ambulance, and I would have."

"Well her carer has been, I saw her, and that friend of hers."

"Oh her. Well she'd have to have her beak in if something was going on."

"That's not very charitable. She comes most days I think."

All heads turned as a car pulled up and what was obviously a doctor got out.

The little crowd was silent as Rosy opened the door and silently beckoned him in.

"I reckon she's gone."

"Sshh. We don't know that."

"Well she has, you mark my words."

They were quiet for a moment then one had a bright idea.

"If that friend of hers is still there, she'll fill us in when she comes out."

"In every minute detail I'll wager."

Although nobody commented, they all knew it was the truth.

Although the high angels had tried to prevent Russ driving to fetch Irene, he had brushed it aside and got into his car but Denzil was on full alert and ready for action.

"Damn and blast. Come on." Russ hit the steering wheel.

The car wouldn't start. After several attempts he gave up, got out and kicked the tyre in temper. What should he do?

"Ah. I'll get a taxi."

As he got out his mobile and started to search for a nearby one, he realised he hadn't got a signal.

"Shit. Shit. Shit."

He almost threw the thing on the ground but something stopped him, making him realise that wouldn't help matters. He locked the car and went back into the house.

As soon as he got into the hall the house phone started to ring so he dashed to it and grabbed it.

"Yes. I mean hello."

It was Irene.

"It's me. Have you left yet?"

He took a deep breath and swallowed the reply he almost gave.

"Car wouldn't start mother. I'm going to get a taxi."

"No. Don't do that. It's alright. That's why I'm ringing."

He refrained from uttering "Well get on with it then."

"That nice carer I told you about, she will bring me home. Wasn't that kind of her?"

"Oh yes. That's good. Thank her won't you."

"Well of course, do you think I've forgotten my manners?"

As he put the handset down, he couldn't help thinking how quickly she seemed to have got over the shock. He would have expected her to still be in tears or at least quieter than she was. But then, would he ever properly understand her?

There are times when decisions are harder to make for the high angels than for the everyday person in the street. If it was inevitable that Irene was going to be terminated as soon as she had passed the evil, at least Russ would not have her in his car when it happened. Also if he was not fetching her by any means, he would not be in danger of being involved in a car accident because it was unknown as to what form her demise would take. It could be anything. The simplest would be a heart attack, but there was no way of knowing. For now, all they could hope for was intervention by 'the others' but they had to rely on whoever could request them. You didn't summon that kind of force.

Denzil's main objective now was to protect his twin. He was ready for anything although he was well enough away not to arouse any suspicions from either side. His guardians were on high alert warning him not to do anything to jeopardise his progress. His reaction was simply "Trust me."

Chapter 10

The vicar sat reading but was aware of his wife's scrutiny.
"You still haven't told me why those people were here."
"My dear, we have been over it hundreds of times. People come to me because they have problems and to be honest, I think you could take a greater part in it. You don't mix, you don't talk to them much apart from the odd 'hello'. Didn't you realise what being a vicar's wife would be like?"
"Ha. And how am I supposed to be able to help. You say many times 'oh it was a personal matter'. So that doesn't include me."
"Look. Some have, well ladies problems, oh I don't mean physical, but they could do with talking to another woman. We have different ways of looking at things and you could have been a great asset, whereas......"
"I am a burden. Why not say it?"
He had to be careful here because whatever he said would be taken the wrong way, chewed over and could go on for days.
"Of course not." He kept it very simple.
There was silence and his mind slipped back to when he was a very eligible bachelor, whom many had tried to catch for themselves or family members but he never met anyone who really took his fancy. Well, there was one but she was already engaged so that was out of the question. As he was getting into his late thirties he thought he would always be alone but then this family moved into his parish and soon he seemed to be seeing a lot of the daughter, not from his doing but hers. Her mother seemed to have decided that they were right for each other as they were a Christian family and she was pure in every way. She made sure he knew that. He thought she wasn't bad looking and would be a nice companion and was entirely suitable to take on

the role of vicar's wife. So they married much to her mother's relief who thought she would be on the shelf forever.

But it didn't take long to realise that this had been a terrible mistake. She wasn't a bad person, nothing evil about her but they really weren't suited. He didn't know what she had been looking for but he certainly wasn't it. Being a clergyman, divorce was out of the question, so they led this boring life together for as long as they were both in body.

She had been selected as part of the clock formation because, in spite of her relationship with her husband, she was basically a good spirit, she just had a funny way of showing it. She had done the job perfectly and it was noticed she had a very strong resistance to any evil that was hovering and could oust them from her area. In fact, her husband couldn't have been in a safer place. It was a pity he felt so much that he was underachieving, for instead of being his rock she was more like a boulder weighing him down.

There are many times that spirits are placed in certain bodies for a reason which may not be obvious at first or even for many years, but they are essential in the general planning of things for future use. Things rarely happen by accident but we are not privy to know the whys and wherefores. For one thing, we do not have the understanding in this life, it is only later when we see part of the overall picture.

This was a textbook situation where spirits in body were often unnoticed and when needed, came into their own. They tended to fade into the background, almost nameless but they could be the most dangerous force to be reckoned with. The vicar was out on visits and his wife sat, hands in her lap with her head bowed. She had been called to help in a situation and although she would remember nothing of it afterwards for her own safety, she would be a very powerful entity who never failed in the task she was set. In many ways she was unequalled.

As she left her physical form she was directed to Lily's house. Immediately she knew the whole story and was aware the Irene was about to leave taking the evil passenger with her and that Russ was still at their home. It only took a second for her to locate and identify the evil presence and before Rosy could even get

Irene into the car, the thing had been despatched to higher forces for them to deal with. Her job done, she returned to her body and was totally unaware of the life she had saved from early termination.

When the vicar returned he would, as always after such tasks, see nothing different about his wife little knowing what an important job she did. Even Sam hadn't picked up on anything like this, so clever was she at being undercover. Of course Violet and Janet just saw her as the most antisocial boring person ever which was just how it was planned. Another case of being hidden in plain sight.

Denzil was relieved that Russ hadn't been taken out of body in this way. Of course he wanted him with him but not through evil intervention, and why should Irene suffer by being pushed over when it wasn't her time? He was full of admiration for the spirit that had dived in, done the job and was gone. Now that's the way he liked to operate. It was all over so quickly that he hadn't had time to identify the presence, but that was essential. She must never be recognised.

Russ put the kettle on while his mum took her coat off. He couldn't help feeling sorry for her but knew she couldn't wait to be the first with the news.

"I'd better tell our Vi." She said as she reached for the phone.

"Did she know her then?" Russ almost smiled as he thought of the women in the clock formation.

"Well she knows she was my friend."

"Oh yes."

He knew she would be kept busy for some time and the thought was put into his head to go and try the car again. He was undecided. If wouldn't start before, why should it now? But at least it would save him having to listen to his mum rattling on and on and on. He went out, tried it, and it started.

"Well stone me." He said, or words to that effect. Without thinking, for some reason he added "Third time lucky."

When he got back indoors he wasn't surprised to find his mum still deep in conversation with someone.

"And I told you she'd been really snappy with me, well that must have been a tumour or something on her brain, because she swore you know. Now you tell me, have you ever heard her do that?"

There was a short silence while the person on the other end had the chance to get a word in. But it didn't last long.

"Well I don't know what she died of, I mean it could have been anything. I expect there will be a post thing or whatever they do."

The call ended and Russ guessed that the other person had reached saturation point.

"Now who's next?"

"Mum." Russ tried to sound understanding. "Why not give it a rest for a bit eh?"

"But there's people who need to know."

"No mum, there's people who you want to be the first to tell. And that's different."

Her face said more than words could. She grabbed her tea, nearly spilling it down her front and made it obvious she wasn't pleased.

Janet had gone round to Violet's for a catch up as they called it. It wasn't long before the recent news was exchanged but as neither knew the lady it didn't affect them that much.

"I bet your sis in law made a meal of it, what with her being there I mean."

Violet laughed. "Try four course meal and you'll be nearer the mark."

After a while Janet asked "I don't suppose you've been past that house lately have you?"

"You mean the one on the corner that we thought was creepy?"

"Yes that one."

"Only going to church. Why?"

"It's just it seemed funny again, but ignore me."

"No come on. You wouldn't mention it unless you'd noticed something."

Janet was hesitant.

"Can't put my finger on it but something is strange. I've seen movements."

Violet laughed.

"Well it's obvious you daft date. Somebody must have moved in."

"Do you know I never thought of that. Oh that must be it. But there was definitely movement."

Violet was suspicious and asked "Hang on a minute. How do you know? I mean where was the movement?"

"In the house of course."

"Have they cut any trees down?"

Janet didn't catch on to why Vi was asking this.

"Not to my knowledge. What's that got to……..oh my god."

"Exactly, you can't see the windows from the road."

There was silence for a minute then Vi asked "You sure it's not just imagination again." Then to lighten the mood "Or had you had a few?"

"No, I'm being silly. Forget it. I am."

They changed the subject but Vi was concerned that Janet had mentioned it because there must have been a good reason and she wondered if her friend was alright.

The angels were satisfied that nothing evil had remained at Lily's house. She had been removed and was 'clean'. The one occupying Irene for a while had been removed and Rosalie was untouched so the place could be spiritually cleansed. One question remained. Where had Lisa gone? But that led onto whether she had taken any evil with her to distribute somewhere else? It would help if they could establish her whereabouts. Even if she was fairly inexperienced she could get in the way, cause distractions to draw the good forces away from what they should be concentrating on. And there was still the ongoing question of who she could be working for at any time. It didn't have to be just one source of evil, the greedy thing would take on anything, or thought she could. But she shouldn't be too hard to locate, unless of course someone was hiding her.

The rest of the day seemed to pass very slowly for some yet had gone in a flash for others. Irene's main concern now was what to wear for church tomorrow because she would obviously be the centre of attention as the word spread and the vicar was going to say a special prayer for Lily. She had thought of asking Russ to come again but she knew he'd refuse and on thinking about it, that wouldn't suit her for he would either say something untoward or want to be hurrying of while she needed to stay as long as possible.

Upstairs he had picked up on her musing and the thought crossed his mind "too right mother, I would have opened my mouth." But what he really needed was a conference with his twin. The 'three' situation was getting stronger and although he was still curious as to who it could be, he was beginning to worry about Denzil's obsession with it for he guessed it could lead to danger.

The vicar had written his sermon for the next day but he wasn't feeling at peace. It was too quiet, not in earthly terms but something was brewing spiritually and it didn't have a good feel about it. He wondered if his wife had something to do with it. The atmosphere in the house had changed earlier but now it seemed to be back to normal. He closed his eyes and put his hands together. He prayed for guidance and the strength to fight anything that threatened life, but most of all he prayed for protection. He wasn't sure why, but he just knew that it had to do it as though his guardian was making him build a protective wall, not only around him but his wife and their home.

Many people, especially those who are spiritually aware always know when something is not right. Everything around them may look the same, but the feeling can be one of unease, or a very strong sense of foreboding. They may not hear about any disaster or misfortune until days later and put it down to premonition. The problem is they won't know what form it will take. It is just a feeling. But taken a step further, why do some feel they must not take a journey and then an accident happens? This is quite common, so when taken to higher levels it can be an advantage, for you know what you are fighting and can take steps to prevent it.

It was this kind of feeling that the vicar was picking up but try as he might to identify it, he couldn't and felt helpless as he knew there was something he should be doing. But what?

He turned his mind to the following day. Although such a short distance he always walked to the church alone, his wife following so that she got there just before the start of any service and she left immediately it had finished. This meant she didn't have to partake in idle gossip. She knew the congregation didn't think it was the thing to do and some didn't mind making a few comments for her to hear but that rolled off her and were ignored.

To say the vicar wasn't happy was an understatement. He finished his prayers and made plans for the afternoon. He would look in on the ladies who were doing the flowers this week as that was always a pleasant atmosphere. He wandered into the garden enjoying the fresh air and admiring how well Sam kept the place. He noticed Violet and Janet going towards the church so called to his wife to tell her where he was going and hurried his pace a little.

"Hello ladies. What have you got for us this week?"

"Hello vicar," Violet showed her blooms. "Thought these would be nice."

"They are very cheerful." He said but looked at her closely. "Are you alright?"

She looked at Janet as if for support.

"Well I am vicar, but my sister in law's friend has died, so of course she is very upset."

"Quite sudden it was." Janet added.

"Sit down for a minute ladies." He beckoned to the front row wondering if this was what had been affecting him. "Do you want to talk?"

Violet answered. "Well we don't know much, but well, Irene, that's my sister in law, does like to elaborate."

"She stirs it." Janet was basic.

The vicar smiled, almost pleased at the aside, but felt there was more here than he may get to know. Something was urging him to stick with it.

"Had the lady been poorly?"

Violet seemed very hesitant.

"Well as far as I can make out mind, she had been housebound but still a character, I mean she was a nice person."

"Which is more than can be said for……" Janet was doing it again so Violet chipped in.

"My sister in law, does tend to um well, shall we say tell you every detail."

"Gossip."

The look Janet got told her to keep it buttoned.

The vicar felt he had to intervene so asked quietly "Sudden then?"

"I'm not sure." Violet didn't want things to come out wrong but there was something pushing her to tell him what she knew, or at least what Irene had told her. "You see she was sort of herself until a day or so then she went, um what did Irene say, oh yes, rude, I mean not vulgar, but harsh, and she says she swore at her. That seemed to go quite deep."

"Oh I see." The vicar had dealt with many cases like this and although something was niggling at him he thought it best to calm the waters so answered "Well, I'm afraid this isn't uncommon. Upsetting as it may be, it isn't really the person you know talking. They are not always coherent, it's a ramble sometimes. They wouldn't want to hurt you in any way."

"Her Irene would." Janet's remark was ignored.

The vicar didn't know why but he was picking up a connection that he couldn't explain, almost as if he had been there.

As soon as the spirits realised that his wife had left a minute disturbance during her visit they erased it immediately and he dismissed it. A lesson had to be learnt here. How ever high or talented a spirit might be, they must always make sure an area was cleansed completely after any operation. It was often impossible to know who had been, but that was unimportant.

After a few more minutes chatting, the vicar felt as though a weight had been lifted and he watched the ladies as they went about their jobs. This was such a welcome change from the atmosphere at home and he decided he must get out more often and even become involved in the various groups. He found Janet a breath of fresh air and it had been hard not to laugh at her comments. That was something else. How often did he actually laugh?

As he made his way back to the vicarage there was a bit of a spring in his step. This would be a new beginning and after all why shouldn't he enjoy life a bit?

If this was observed by the good angels, it certainly wasn't missed by the evil onlookers. Now they could have some fun and they had just the candidate for it. A bit of scandal was just what they loved and to bring a vicar into disrepute was even better.

The hierarchy were still monitoring Denzil and if he didn't tow the line soon, he would forego his only chance to ascend. On a total recall, if you mess up, that's it. You don't just float away into paradise, you have to work for it and prove you are worthy.

He was trying to mask his thoughts and knowledge but those on the high levels could see straight through him. They were aware that he was trying to urge Russ to find number three and they knew that couldn't happen, for where the third one had been originally in a previous life, could be anywhere now, that is if they were still in existence. On occasions the ultra evil were terminated and every particle spread beyond realms of our understanding. So it could be a dead end and who would explain it to Denzil? But it was still a possibility.

Russ lay on his bed, mulling over the events of the day but still the word was hammering. Three. Three Three. If only he could find the answer, his twin would be content. But then the doubt crept in. Why was it so important? What if he did locate the third one, he may regret it for eternity. Couldn't Denzil just forget it and progress naturally? He knew he couldn't tell him this for he wouldn't listen.

The good angels were really working on Russ's subconscious now. If they could put a block here, Denzil would hopefully be forced to go elsewhere knowing this was a dead end but it could damage their close relationship. It was suggested that if he thought that much of him he wouldn't keep pestering him, but he was turning into a desperate entity and soon he would be passed the point of progression, simply because he wouldn't be fit or suitable to be elevated.

Russ's attention was turned to the following day, and church. What on earth would his mother have planned for that? Well, whatever it was she'd milk it dry. Thank, goodness he wasn't going to be there to see it. With those thoughts, he drifted gently off to sleep.

Denzil was furious. Something was intercepting and preventing Russ from searching for the missing 'three'. Yes, spirits get angry and throw a strop when things don't go their way, but as on earth it is often self destructive and produces the opposite results to what they are trying to achieve. And he was heading straight down this path. But was it time for him to get help from other sources? Then it came to him. He remembered when he had seen that Lisa before! It was many decades ago and she was in male form then but they had enjoyed an alliance. If she was still the little rogue she/he had been, she would be the prime candidate to help, but he had to find her first.

Little did he know, he wouldn't have long to wait, but she had another assignment first unless of course she was clever enough to take on two jobs. Things were going to get very interesting especially when he remembered one thing. She or whatever form she used was one of the 'you scratch mine and I'll scratch yours' brigade, and nothing would have changed there, you could put money on it.

Chapter 11

There was a stillness in the air when Sunday dawned. There was no sun, no wind and even the birds were not at their usual volume. Irene made the first tea of the day and called up to Russ that his was on the table as she had no intention of running up and down stairs when he was capable of coming down himself. She was aware he'd not felt well but she didn't always feel up to the mark but had to carry on, and she was a bit peeved that he seemed to have almost forgotten that her friend had died. However, she brightened up at the thought of going to church and spreading the tale in full after the service. She was determined to get her money's worth out of this one and it was almost ironic that the very one she had been going to see for gossip was the one who, in the end provided her with it.

Russ appeared and without word, took his tea and slumped in the armchair.

"I suppose it's too much to ask if you are coming to give me support today?" She fiddled in her handbag so she didn't have to look at him as she hated some of his glances.

"You know very well I'm not," he almost whispered "and you can manage perfectly well without support from anyone."

She wanted to appear as though she had ignored him and said "What are you going to do with yourself today then?"

He just shrugged, so she tried her usually route.

"Well I'll tell you what you are doing tomorrow my lad. You are going to see the doctor and find out just what's wrong with you." Then under her breath added "If there is such a condition as bone idleness."

He stood up, faced her and said very quietly "Perhaps you would have rather I died". And left the room, but he had noticed the shock on her face as he fired his little arrow.

The vicar had left for church before his wife as usual but today he had a spring in his step. Nothing was going to drag him down to the depths of despair again and starting from now, he was going to start appreciating all the wonders of nature that were around him. Negative thoughts were banned. Of course, as a clergyman he would have to deal with other people's problems including bereavement but he could handle that as it was his job. What he wasn't going to do was let anything bring any despair into his own life. He would be a dutiful and faithful husband, whatever that meant, for there was no love or intimate physical contact between them. Sometimes his body ached for a bit of relief, but she certainly had no intention of doing anything about it, and he daren't speak about it as she told him he was rude. There were times when he wished he'd been a monk.

As he entered the church and made his way to the vestry he acknowledged the greeters who were always early and in position. Then he noticed one of the congregation sitting near the back on her own and she was a stranger. He wanted to go back and ask the helpers who she was but that would have seemed a bit obvious so he just inclined his head by way of acknowledgment. He may have looked calm on the outside but as she looked at him, his inside gave a jolt. She was stunning. In this job you got used to meeting new people, visitors, some who stayed for a while then left but they didn't stand out like this one. He got to the safety of the vestry, glad to be out of sight for the encounter was having a definite effect on him and it took every ounce of will power to calm it down. He just hoped his parts would behave all the way through the service! Then he remembered his wife would be sitting in the front row and in a way that did the trick.

Violet and Janet arrived along with all the regulars and the service seemed to flow along until they got to the sermon. He had his notes, but put them down and spoke without even glancing at them for he was going to change his original theme. All of a sudden he was going to speak about taking stock of your life and sometimes stopping to think. Are you just drifting along with the flow because that's how life is or do you accept that your own destiny is in your hands? If the answer is yes, what are you going to do about it. Not tomorrow, not next week or next year. Now.

There was a hush. He daren't look towards his wife and his attention was drawn to the back of the church. At least one person was completely in tune with him and the message that came to him didn't need any words for her intentions were absolutely clear. He had the strangest feeling that this was all planned from somewhere else and he had no say in it, but must follow his instincts for his new life. Never before had anything like this happened but somehow he didn't question any part of it. This was his new path and he would travel it.

The service ended normally and as they left, people were saying how profound the sermon was and perhaps they could learn from it. His wife had left almost straight away, as was her norm, but it was obvious she would either have plenty to say to him when he got home, or he would be met with a wall of silence. Strangely enough it didn't worry him any more.

The new person was one of the last to leave and as he shook her hand, he felt something was put into his. She didn't hang around and left fairly quickly but he knew he would see her again, and it would be very soon.

When there is a small and regular congregation, anyone new stands out and it is the usual practice to make them feel welcome. Janet had soon gone to ask the newcomer if she would like to sit with them but all she got was a slight smile and the reply that she was alright where she was. Followed by a polite 'thank you'.

As Violet couldn't ask her much in church, as soon as they left she wanted to know what she had said as it had been so quick.

"Didn't want to know." Was Janet's reply. "But I did notice where her attention was."

"Oh yes?"

"Well, she seemed to have our vicar in her sights, and nobody else. And did you notice how she hung back and held his hand when he went to shake hers?"

"No because I was talking to the ones from the knitting group. Oh, I missed it." She sounded quite disappointed.

"Don't worry, you'd had to have been quick. But...well.. no I shouldn't think things."

Violet took her arm in a confidential way.

"I'm always interested when you 'think things' as you put it. Come on. Spill."

Janet laughed.

"Do you know, I think you are as bad as your sister in law when it comes to something that smacks of being juicy."

"Well, you're going to tell me anyway." She laughed.

"Oh I don't know exactly, but you know when you get a gut instinct that you've met someone before?"

"You know her?"

"No, No not me. Him. I felt they knew each other already, although he did look a bit surprised to see her."

"Ooo, I bet he did. And what about his missus?"

"Well, she hadn't arrived when he first saw this new one and she'd left before the handshake bit."

Violet was enjoying this and her cheeky side was coming to the surface.

"Well he wouldn't want her to see his handshake would he?"

Janet sputtered.

"You are awful. You know very well what I meant, mind you….."

They had just passed the empty house almost without realising it and were exchanging a more innuendos when Janet stopped.

"Do you realise something?"

"What?" Violet was hoping she hadn't missed anything important.

"Just stop for a moment."

"Ok." Violet wondered what her friend was up to.

"Listen."

"I can't hear anything, well that car that just went by, oh and a dog barked but nothing else."

"Exactly. We've had our minds on other things and that house has had no effect on us whatsoever."

Violet looked at the leaves just moving slightly. All was calm.

"You mean, there was nothing spooky there all the time?"

Janet walked on slowly.

"It's just that I was watching a programme on telly. It was all about the mind and how you can make people believe something that isn't right. Some are experts at it."

"So are you saying that people made up something and we believed it, because that isn't how it was?" Violet was adamant. "It was a feeling, a creepy feeling that I was being watched and nobody had said anything before about the place. Don't you remember, we both noticed it."

Janet seemed to fob it off with "Oh well, there's obviously nothing to worry about and we've got more interesting things to keep our eyes on."

They parted with different feelings. Janet was on a high but Violet sensed something wasn't right and felt her friend was being a bit too interested in something that wasn't her business and that could spell trouble.

The vicar said goodbye to the church warden and the couple who were getting ready things for Sunday school and walked very happily to the vicarage.

"Oh hello Sam, didn't expect to see you." He jumped as the man suddenly appeared as he was nearing the little gate.

"Morning vicar." Sam looked at him closely and removed his cap. "Good sermon. Look after yourself."

Replacing his cap he walked away, but there seemed to be something unusual in his manner.

"Hope he's alright." Vicar thought as he entered the house.

His wife was in the kitchen and he wasn't going to wait to see if she was in one of her silent moods so he spoke first.

"Very pleasant out isn't it. I enjoyed the little walk. Perhaps I should go out more. It would be healthier."

She may have appeared to be ignorant of anything that had occurred at church but in fact she had been pre-warned and was way ahead of them.

Now she turned to face him and said "We used to go for some very nice walks. Maybe we should take it up again. What a good idea of yours."

That was the last thing he expected and knocked him back a bit. Here was a dilemma. He was planning to get away on his own for a while and she had thrown a large spanner in that plan, and then turned it round as though he had suggested it. Unfortunately, he wasn't quick enough to wriggle out of that one and so he just agreed, for now at least.

But evil operators are not put off by minor hiccups and his admirer had already planned for such things. Suddenly he remembered that the new visitor had passed something to him so he went to the toilet where he could see what it was. He carefully unfolded the small note which simply said "I'm waiting."

Not being one for clandestine meetings, he had no idea how to handle this. Was he supposed to answer? He thought that maybe she would make the next move but then something in his mind pulled him up short. Warning bells were going off and if he had known who was ringing them he would have been even more shocked. This was too much to take in so he decided to forget all about it for now. It was some silly female trying to seduce him and he didn't need that kind of complication. Then he thought of his new carefree life. If this was anything to go by, he may have to think again. The powers protecting him were working and they were in close proximity although he was totally unaware of them. Together they put a protective force around him but when an evil doer has made up their mind, nothing will stop them in their quest.

Irene had worn her black coat today as a mark of respect and gone off to church leaving Russ to feel sorry for himself, as she put it. This was an ideal opportunity for Denzil to contact his twin without interference, at least from the physical side but the two would not be alone, the high levels had seen to that. He had planned that he would keep the matter of 'three' well away from his thoughts so they wouldn't be interrupted. He started by referring to the recall and the fact that although it had been believed Lisa may have opened a portal for evil to enter, the idea had been disregarded.

"Are you saying the evil entered anyway, even if it wasn't her?" Russ asked.

"Not necessarily. It may have been planned but nothing strong has been let loose. She isn't of a high enough standing to do it anyway."

"Oh? How do you know?"

Denzil was keeping away from his true reason.

"Think I've met her before. Bit vague though."

Russ may not have felt well but his senses were working overtime.

"And are you going to tell me, or are you going to be secretive?"

Denzil was fighting to keep the reason out of his thinking but he could feel Russ almost boring into his thoughts.

"Look, nothing to concern yourself about. He is trash."

"Well which is it?"

"Come again."

"Is it she, or is it he?"

Denzil fobbed his error off with "Well you know we flit from one to the other in out earth lives, and yes she was male at one point, as far as I can remember. Not important."

Russ's guards put a big question mark into his thoughts. Why was his friend here? He wasn't at ease and this wasn't casual. There had to be a purpose or he would have been popping in and out as usual.

"And so, what is it you are trying to impart?" He came straight out with it.

"Not with you." Denzil tried to sound confused.

Russ paused before laying it out.

"Why is this Lisa person even worthy of mention if she or he is so inexperienced. Plus you haven't got round to the usual subject. I guess there is a tie. How am I doing so far?"

Denzil was not expecting this response and could tell his partner was getting too close to the truth.

"Ok. So what have you come up with? Nothing and time is running out."

It was Russ's turn to be angry.

"Just look at yourself. You have all the skills to ascend and what are you doing with them. Wasting them on a futile quest, to which I might add you will never know the answer and you can't accept it is for your own good."

"You know." Denzil would have screamed had he been in physical. "You've known all along and yet you won't tell me."

"I will say for the last time, I have never known, I don't want to know and if that's all you've come for, you've wasted your precious time. So good luck with your little underling because she won't find out for you, she can't. You are just throwing away your total recall, so if you have an ounce of sense left you will concentrate on that and forget your obsession, or you will live in hell."

Whether or not it was the right thing to do, the guardians were pushing Russ to explode and come out with his innermost feelings. It had one immediate effect, for Denzil had gone as though he had never been there.

Anger is a destructive power but it was what was driving Denzil to contact Lisa now and set her to work. Russ had been right about one thing, she couldn't help him, but in his state he wouldn't accept it and she would take any job if it was to her advantage and gave her leverage for the future. Denzil had remembered correctly, she certainly was a back scratcher.

It took him seconds to locate her near the vicarage. He took on a different image as he approached.

"Want a job beautiful?"

"Depends. I'm in great demand. What is it?"

"I need a nosey one. Someone that isn't afraid to get their spirit dirty."

"Do I know you?"

He was on the alert. Surely she hadn't twigged.

"Doubt it. I've heard you do a bit of business sometimes, but if you're not bothered, there's plenty more who will jump at it. I need someone experienced anyway. See you."

"No wait. I have got something on but it will keep."

He'd got her interest but the next question was inevitable.

"What's in it for me?"

He had to make this so she couldn't refuse.

"More power than you can imagine. And believe me, nobody will ever get the better of you again. You will be feared."

Now he had got her but she still wanted reassurance.

"How do I know you can give me this power?"

"Oh I don't. It comes from much higher, but when they see what you are capable of, they will amply reward you, I can assure you of that."

"Well, I've only got your word for it." She was tempted and not one to pass up a chance.

He decided to plant the final seed.

"You see, this is what I do. I go out and find suitable talent. I'm just a scout but I get rewarded if I come up with the goods, so you see we both benefit."

"Oh, you're only like an agent. I get it. That makes sense. And who's your boss?"

"Hey come on. We never see them. We get the clients, then we get the rewards. It works well, and you get the extra power, now that's the bit I like. Want some proof?"

"You can do that?"

"Sorry, I'm being summoned, something big." He'd gone.

She thought for a moment. This was too good to miss but she wished she'd found out what the job was. She wasn't sure if she'd agreed or not as everything was churning round and then something else jolted her memory. She didn't recognise him but there was the slightest familiarity about him. She had to find out who he was. But for the moment she had to deal with her current task. She had to seduce the vicar and make him sin big time.

The scene outside another church was completely different. It was Irene who was holding the attention and enjoying every minute of it. She was so wrapped up in relaying every detail that she failed to notice that some were drifting away discussing how false she was coming over.

"She's got no respect for her friend."

"Just wants the glory for herself. As usual."

"And we don't even know if everything that's she's saying is right."

"Oh well you can bet your sweet life she's glorified it to the hilt."

One of them giggled.

"I wonder what her friend actually thought of her."

"Probably not a friend anyway, some poor thing who was a captive audience you might say."

The remaining listeners were either too polite to leave or were the ones that Irene relied on, fellow gossip mongers and they knew how to keep her going until they had the last dregs to mull over.

"Had you known her long then?" One asked.

"Oh yes. Years, but don't ask me to count or I will feel old." This was how she got out of most things.

"When is the funeral? Of course you will be going."

"Well of course. I mean I was there when she...."

She patted her eyes with her hanky, one of her best ones of course and side tracked the first question she hoped. But it was repeated.

"Oh it's far to early to say, I mean there's all the paperwork isn't there and the family will see to it but they will tell me as soon as they know."

"What family has, I mean had she?"

Now she was on a spot because she knew very little about Lily's private life so she had to think quickly.

"Well the undertaker is looking into all that so I kept out of it, I mean there is a certain amount of privacy at times like this."

The little audience had just about dispersed knowing she had almost come to the end of her performance and couldn't milk it any further.

As she made her way home, the 'high' that she had been on was rapidly diminishing as she felt the apprehension of seeing Russ. He was draining her and seemed to be drifting more into his private world. She seriously considered asking his doctor if the problem wasn't physical, but mental. That would be a disgrace and she wouldn't want anyone to know because of the stigma attached so she may only go down that route if absolutely necessary.

"He's just run down." She decided as she let herself in but was met with a shock.

He had got everything ready for dinner as usual and was checking the meat as she walked in.

"Oh. This is a nice surprise. I thought you might still be in bed."

"I'm feeling better Mum. Whatever bug it was, has gone. I feel more like myself now."

"Well I'm very glad to hear it and I hope you don't get it again, that's all I can say."

She was looking round for something to do but he seemed to have covered everything. The table was laid, the plates were warming and he'd even made the gravy.

"You know Mum, sometimes things, or people can get you down and they control you although you don't realise it. You daren't say the wrong thing, or do something they don't approve of or you will bloody well suffer for it. Well, there comes a time when you find the strength to stand up and say that you aren't a dogsbody and you don't have to take it anymore because they are crushing you and you have to be yourself."

You could have heard a pin drop. They both stood in silence for a moment but it was obvious that he meant every word he said.

"I didn't know you thought of me that way." Her voice held a sadness.

He laughed. "Not you, I know how to handle you."

Her face changed at that remark and would have been funny if she hadn't taken it so seriously so he tried to explain.

"Mum, how can I put it? Somebody can become so part of your life or part of you that you don't question anything, you just go along with it because you think they must be right. But then they may do something that you don't agree with and you step back and have a good look at the overall picture."

"I think I see. Has somebody treated you that way, only you don't tell me much."

He laughed.

"Mum, there's a lot of things men don't share with their mothers."

She was pensive when she said sadly "Pity your dad hasn't been here for you. Now he'd have had none of it, I can tell you,."

"It's ok Mum. Everything will be ok now. Promise."

He gave her a little hug which surprised her but she welcomed it all the same.

"Right, let's have this dinner. It smells lovely." She smiled.

He couldn't help thinking how things near to him had changed dramatically in the last few hours. But now he was his own person, and not relying on anyone else.

For the time being he was going to sit back and watch, for if Denzil did find out the truth about 'three', it would be something not to be missed, but could mean the end of Denzil's total recall. He had an idea of what had taken place in the past but it was only a supposition which was why he couldn't give any clue to it as there had been many possibilities. The fact that Denzil has almost hounded him thinking that he knew the answer had driven a wedge between them but it wasn't of his doing. This is what had upset him but then something, or someone had given him the power to fight back, not against Denzil but for himself. He hoped that he wouldn't visit him again, and sometime soon it would be obvious to him that his so called 'twin' had be truthful all along.

Chapter 12

The high angels were asking a lot of questions. They had suspected Lisa of using the clock formation as a means for a strong evil to enter the area but now they were beginning to look at it from many angles. She wasn't strong enough herself to do it so she would have to be employed from a higher source who would use her simply to appear to unlock the door so they could invade under their own power. If that were the case, who were they, and more importantly where? The next suggestion was that all this was a decoy for a bigger operation and while everyone was trying to trace this evil, there was nothing to find because it was operating elsewhere but nobody would know until it struck, and by then it would be too late.

She was just a tool to be used and now she had the possibility of two jobs to keep her busy for a while. She would enjoy the vicar project but was totally unaware that there was a strong guardian ready to block her, his wife. It was obvious Denzil had dangled the carrot and she would take the bait when he returned as she craved power, and that was what he seemed to be offering. Something was niggling and although she wanted answers, it wouldn't put her off. What was it that had jolted her memory? She always liked to place people and she couldn't with him so either they had met many earth lives before, or they had been very close and he didn't want her to know. When someone starts playing these games there has to be a good reason. Her thoughts were computing and she wanted answers. She was cautious to an extent but power seekers have such a thirst to be dominant and that's what drives them.

Questions. Has he something to hide? What did he look like if I knew him?

What does he want now? Did he seek me out specially or is he playing the field?

Then another thought hit her.

"Oh bloody hell! He thinks I'm Leon."

What many didn't remember was, that at first there were twins and although Lisa had become well known for her evil connections, Leon seemed to have faded into obscurity almost immediately. It wasn't Lisa with whom Denzil had shared and alliance, it was Leon. This wouldn't affect her decision because she already had the vicar to service and she needed the physical connection to satisfy her reminder of happy moments, but she would take Denzil's job for her own advancement. It could prove very interesting especially as she wouldn't enlighten him but let him realise for himself. She wondered what the information was that he wanted her to find. Now that couldn't be passed by because when you were looking into other people's secrets, it was amazing what else you could come up with on the way. Then you had plenty of bargaining power in other situations, oh yes, she would enjoy this. The thought came to her that she didn't know when she would encounter him again. He had just left her in a flash but if the job was important to him, and he couldn't do it himself, he'd be back.

It was Sunday afternoon and the vicar was on his way back from the Sunday school. As he approached the little gate he saw the familiar figure of the newcomer obviously waiting for him. Everything stirred inside him again but he didn't want to give any idea that she was having such an effect on him.

"Oh I hope you didn't mind vicar but you see I have to talk to somebody urgently, that is, someone who won't say anything."

"My dear, that's what I'm here for and of course confidentiality is an essential part of my work."

Sam happened to be walking past at that moment and he touched his cap.

"Afternoon miss, afternoon vicar."

His pace slowed almost to a stop. The vicar acknowledged his greeting but Lisa ignored him, her eyes holding the vicar's attention but he was feeling very uncomfortable and something was almost dragging him away.

"Perhaps you'd like to make an appointment." He suggested.

She sensed the defences going up and moved so close she was touching him but her face turned towards Sam with such a stare, he moved away.

"I don't make appointments vicar. If I have something that needs attention now, it means now."

Her hands were just creeping round his neck when Sam coughed loudly and said "I think you are wanted vicar."

Lisa's voice cut through the air.

"How observant of you, now go and play somewhere else."

If it hadn't been the vicar she was mauling, she would have said "piss off".

"Oh not me miss. Her."

A broad grin was across his face as he indicated towards the vicarage where the vicar's wife stood also with a beaming smile.

"I deal with all female problems miss, perhaps you had better make an appointment with me."

Lisa was furious.

"And you are also a vicar are you?"

"What is more important, I am his wife, and you can take your hands with your common fingernails off his person."

It was one of those situations when the air was so loaded, nobody moved for a moment and it was a battle of wills. There was a funny side to it for Sam gradually sidled in until he was grinning up at Lisa only inches from her face, the vicar disentangling himself now feeling quite flaccid, the wife with a sarcastic smile and unflinching in her manner. That left Lisa. She had no option but to walk away from the vicarage and although she may appear beaten, her anger rose to such an extent that she knew everyone would suffer as a result of it. The vicar didn't notice the fleeting exchange between Sam and the wife but it had worked well and they were pleased with the result.

The hierarchy were a little confused with Denzil's actions. He would know he was on full monitor constantly, so why attempt to hire a novice to do an expert's work. Then there was the fact that although she didn't know yet what he was going to ask her to do, the watchers certainly would. She could never find his 'three' for him and it would not only be allowing her to discover facts she shouldn't, but give her a contact on levels she hadn't achieved, which was always disastrous often ending in the spirit never having a base which left them vulnerable. Then there was the fact that she was considered evil, not of the worst kind but enough for some to use her for their dirty work. There were two options available. They could either send Denzil to total recall now, but as he wasn't in the right spiritual state that couldn't happen, or they could leave him to his own devices. In the past he had often appeared to go off the rails but had exposed things they weren't even aware of.

Violet and Janet were on their way to evensong and the topic of conversation soon turned to the newcomer.

"She's after him," Janet said almost knowingly, "and she'll have him."

"You don't know that." Vi was often amused by her friend's summary of any situation.

"Oh, you mark my words. She'll be swinging on his bell rope, you see."

"I'd rather not." Vi had to laugh at the very idea of it.

Janet was deep in thought for a moment.

"You know something, it's been bugging me all day."

"What? Apart from her swinging…..ha ha." She couldn't finish the sentence for laughing.

"No. You think about it. If some bloke was sitting there when we walked in, and you didn't know him, what would you do?"

Vi was tempted to say she wouldn't swing on any part of him but instead answered "Well, we'd say 'Good Evening', to make him feel welcome."

"But you wouldn't flash your bits at him."

"Apart from them not being worth looking at, and we would be in a church, and…."

Janet butted in. "You'd just speak, like you said."

"What are you rabbiting on about?"

"Ok. But what if you had known him in the past, very well and I mean very, very, well." She gave a knowing little cough which was like a nudge, nudge, wink, wink. Full of inuendo.

"Hey, what are you suggesting. Not with our vicar."

Janet was just smirking.

"Be a bit different then wouldn't it?"

Violet wanted to bring her out of this moment of fantasy.

"Just come back down to earth a minute. Because she was doing all the enticing, or whatever you want to call it, it doesn't mean a thing. I bet she does it to everyone."

"And how many more men's hands did she hold as she left?" Janet knew she was right and wouldn't let go.

They had reached the church and she almost dragged Vi in to see if the female was there.

"Well blow me down. She's not here yet?" It was supposed to be a whisper but came out as bit louder than expected.

Vi was almost relieved for she was dreading the whole service if her friend's concentration was going to be elsewhere.

"Told you," she whispered, "she's not coming."

Although disappointed Janet had to find a reason.

"Well perhaps she made arrangements to see him somewhere else."

The vicar was pretty sure the female wouldn't dare show her face after the afternoon's episode and breathed a sigh of relief when he saw the space she had occupied in the morning was empty. But Lisa had other plans and she wasn't one to be fobbed off by him, his wife or his gardener. You didn't upset her or make her look silly and not pay for it. It was time for what she enjoyed most. Revenge.

Denzil had been mapping out his movements but being careful to only let certain things be monitored. He had built up the art of being covert to the extent that no-one on any level could hack into his thoughts. This annoyed the hierarchy who were known to be able to hear all, see all, and know all. Although continual attempts had been made to infiltrate, none had succeeded. He had the power to delete incidents, operations, and anything he didn't want to be connected to him from his entire being. But he knew how to retrieve them on his inner spiritual hard drive. There was no doubt that he was a good power as had been proved by his track record, but the question had often been raised as to why he hadn't gone into total recall before. He certainly had a will of his own but you always wondered what was going on under his 'public image', the one he portrayed but was suspected to be altogether different to the real one.

He was now following Lisa and had scanned her memories so he tied up Leon with his own records. There was a strange comparison with the way her twin had become extinct so quickly and the one he called 'three' who also disappeared as though he had never been there. And nobody wanted to talk about it. Perhaps some light would be shed on it before too long.

"Oh it's you." Was her greeting.

"Yes, don't get up." Was his sarcastic reply.

"Oh, who's pulled your chain grumpy?"

Ignoring her he carried on.

"It's a missing persons for the want of a better description."

"Oh yeah?" She was a bit disillusioned. "That all?"

He wasn't going to be treated like a bit of dirt by this creature who needed him.

"Well if it's beneath you, don't bother." And he was gone.

"No, come back, I mean, who is it?"

There was silence.

"Oh bleeding arseholes!" Echoed round the area which attracted a few mischievous entities who hooked on immediately eager for entertainment.

After a few moments Denzil was back but she couldn't make out just where he was.

"Well, you don't seem to be making much progress in your freelance work do you?" The works echoed all around her. She spun to try and pin point them but they were all over the area.

"Stop playing your games." Her whole self screamed.

"And you stop acting like a spoilt child. Now listen. I will give you one attempt at this job and if you cock it up you are out. Do you understand?"

"I'm not an idiot."

There was silence and it was obvious she had to play ball.

"Yes, I understand." But added "You've got to tell me what the payment is before I start."

"Of course. I'm not an idiot." The tone was electric.

"Ok then."

"First. What I want you to do. You need to regress and go to when Russ was first on earth. I want you to go through every contact, every relationship and I want the names of everyone and I mean also nick names, pseudonyms, everything. When you've done one life, you move only the next and you need to cross reference all the time to see who has been making regular connections. Is that clear."

"It's clear."

"If and when you come back with the goods, and they have been proven, you will be elevated to a higher level."

"And what does that mean?" She wanted all the details.

"You don't know? Where have you been?" He then played his joker. "If you have to ask that, I wonder if you are competent enough for this. I really thought you would jump at it. Most do."

"I am, I just wanted to be sure you weren't pulling my chain." She hadn't a clue but daren't admit it now.

"So you will do it!" It wasn't a question. "Believe me you won't regret it, if you pull it off that is. You don't get paid if you haven't delivered of course. Nobody does. Not for something this important."

"It'll be a doddle. Anyone could do it." She wanted to come over as competent which amused him. Then as an after thought "Oh by the way, how long have I got?"

He appeared to be in thought as though he was computing.

"Oh there's no rush. In earth time, let's say tomorrow." And he had gone.

Her next explosion needn't be printed but goes without saying it was colourful to the extreme.

This exchange had been witnessed from above. There were questions about what he thought he was playing at and why didn't he leave things alone? A few were afraid of what may come to light that had no connection to this case, but you don't find out one bit of information without it being attached to another. This is why many things are left unsolved because of embarrassing implications. Nothing is ever lost or not recorded somewhere and how ever much anyone thinks it is dead and buried so to speak, there is always the chance it will rear its ugly head through another source. There would be many souls not resting for a while and plans were being made to stop Lisa digging in the wrong places. In the spirit world you can't just leave to escape scandal, because wherever you go it has already attached itself to you.

Denzil had created such an unrest in all spheres, which was just what he had planned.

When the service had ended, Janet held onto Violet's arm and whispered "We aren't in a hurry are we?" Followed by a knowing little nod.

"Aren't we? Oh I see." And thought, "she is worse than Irene."

They casually put their hymn books back on the pile and turned to say 'Goodnight' to the vicar. They were last in the queue just as Janet had planned.

"That was a lovely sermon vicar."

"Thank you Janet." He smiled "And Violet."

After shaking both their hands he pulled back to return to the vestry but Janet wasn't finished yet.

"I rather thought that friend of yours would be here tonight vicar."

Violet was embarrassed at the forthright approach and tried to drag her friend away but she wasn't having any of it.

"Um, friend?" The vicar tried to look unmoved.

"Yes, you know the one who was here this morning."

Violet could see the vicar was uncomfortable and cut in "Well, must be going vicar. Good night."

He gratefully seized the opportunity and went to the vestry.

Janet's face was a picture and she wasn't going to let Vi get away with the interruption just when she could have found out who the tart was.

"What did you think you were playing at? I'd got him."

"No you hadn't Janet. You were simply embarrassing him and if that woman is making life unpleasant in any way, it's not our business."

The walk home was quite strained and before they parted Violet stopped and said "Just what is your interest? You're not normally so nosey."

"Me, nosey?" The tone was one of annoyance.

136

"Look, we all like a bit of casual gossip now and then and it's harmless but you seem to be hooked onto this one. Now come on, just what's getting at you?"

There was a pause then she said very quietly "You'll just say I'm imagining things."

"No I won't. Why not come back to mine and have a cuppa." Janet thought for a moment then agreed.

"Ok. Probably not a bad idea, but you're not to mock."

"Promise."

When they had settled with a drink and a piece of homemade cake, Violet looked straight at her and said "Go on, and I promise I will take whatever you are going to tell me in all seriousness. Yes?"

"Ok but it will sound a bit strange."

She put her plate down and took a deep breath.

"I know I do daft things but there are times when things happen in my head that I can't understand." She paused for a minute. "I've never said but I get strange feelings."

"What kind of feelings, do you mean premonition type things?"

Janet looked a bit easier at that.

"Yes. But not what people would think."

"Go on. I'm interested."

"Well… it's not that I know what's going to happen to people, you know what I'm saying. It's more, I don't know how to put it so it doesn't sound silly."

Violet surprised her by saying "It's more like you are remembering or seeing what's already happened."

"That's it! You've got it, but hang on. How do you know that?"

"Now you've put me in a spot. I don't know exactly but sometimes, like when we are walking to church, it's as though we've done it before. Yes I know we often do that route, but it's different."

"Oh you've taken a weight of my mind. I thought I was going crazy, I really did."

"Well what if I told you that the vicar's wife looks at us differently to the others."

"No! You mean she thinks we are after her old man?" Janet's eyes were popping out.

Violet had to laugh.

"No and this is something else I can't work out, it's a searching look but it's not nasty. More like we know something that nobody else does."

"Bloody hell fire!"

Vi laughed. "Remember who we are talking about."

"Oh sorry lady." Janet had to laugh too.

The tone was certainly lighter and they were both relieved that they had experienced the same things so they didn't feel odd any more. But there was another side to it. Violet thought it was now time to broach it.

"Tell me, what sort of feeling did you get from that tart woman then?"

"Oh yes, her. Well I know I've never seen her before but....."

"We both have haven't we?"

"You too. But why didn't you say?" Janet demanded.

"Did you?"

"Well no, but you see I wasn't sure then but now you've said it, that's it. I recognised her from somewhere, but I had the feeling she didn't look the same."

"Because I think we knew her as a different person, and maybe from a long time ago. And I'll tell you something else. She knew us."

"What?" Janet wanted to know more. "How can you tell?"

Violet had to slow her down as bit.

"Just a minute. When you walked through this door you were half afraid to tell me how you felt."

"Well I wasn't exactly sure, in my own mind."

"Right. That's how I am now. There is something ....but I don't know...can't place it. I'm probably imagining stuff but Sam looked at us very closely this morning."

"Him too?" Janet stared at her for a minute before she went back into her usual self. "Bloody hell, is there anyone who isn't peering at us. Have we grown two heads or something?"

Soon they were in fits of laughter which lightened the mood and ultimately slipped into girlish jokes and naughty remarks about having two of anything.

They may not have felt quite so relaxed if they had known the amount of attention they had drawn to themselves from various sources.

The high angels realised that, if an evil power had been using the clock formation as a portal, it could easily share everyone's identity merely by planting the thought in those it wished. If Lisa had knowingly or unwittingly opened the door, the first one they could use would be her and anywhere she went or anyone she was in contact with even briefly, would pick it up even if they couldn't place her. It was a strong possibility that this was what was happening to Violet and Janet, and they were getting glimpses of their visits to the vicarage. This would also explain why the good spirits had to spring into action even if it meant temporarily exposing themselves. The vicar's wife and Sam had rallied and the vicar hadn't been surprised. Also it had to be remembered that since Lisa's arrival on the scene, Lily had died.

Another factor had to be addressed. Was it only Irene's connection to Violet that had drawn Lisa to that particular location? After all she was at position ten, and had moved to nine so it could have been her intention to move closer or she may have had another target. To be certain, a thorough check of where all the other clock positions had been was carried out but came up with nothing. Therefore it had to be estimated that she was in this area for a purpose. One of the hierarchy was pretty certain that she was being used because of her low status in order attract attention by cocking up every job she did while the high power would carry out its own plan in secret. And that could be almost anything.

They were also aware that Denzil was keeping her employed on his own useless quest and they wished he would give up and get out of the picture and stop taking her attention as this could be hampering the end result.

Vinn had been in continual presence and observed all that was going on. Russ was glad to have him around but had to be on constant alert to remember to drop his spiritual level when communicating with him. When he was on higher ones, Vinn just accepted he was meditating, little guessing what was really going on.

"Denzil must be busy." He suggested.

Russ thought for a moment before he answered.

"Yes. He does that sometimes. That's the trouble with these higher bods, you never know where they are." He smiled to himself thinking, 'if only you knew'.

"I think he has changed."

Russ wondered about the train of thought so answered cautiously.

"You mean recently?"

"Well yes, and can I say you are different with him?"

Russ had been ready for this for Vinn wasn't stupid.

"Well you know I'm not at my best when I'm in body and he is just in spirit because there is always a barrier. Both on one plane is perfect but it doesn't always happen as you know. When are you due again?" He tried to veer him off attention on himself.

"We never know do we? I've got a couple more to go yet. I like it when I'm in body but I think I will be happier when they are finished."

Russ thought then said "Grass is always greener." Which thankfully brought the discussion to an end for a moment.

With the summer nights it was light until quite late and the vicar liked to sit in his garden and watch the birds going to roost and the odd bat flitting around. His mind turned to the female and he felt ashamed that he had felt an attraction to her. Maybe this new feeling of freedom wasn't so good after all. And his wife! He didn't think he had ever seen her like that, and she seemed to have a different look about her.

"I shouldn't stay out too late, it can get chilly about now." She called through the window.

"I was just coming in."

He was almost afraid to go. How would she be for she could change in a minute and could have gone back to her old self? Well there was only one way to find out. Slowly he picked up his things and stepped into the house.

"I've made us some hot chocolate. Do you want it here or have it in bed?" her voice called from the kitchen.

"Oh, um, shall we have it in the sitting room?"

He thought that would be the best for now so went to the kitchen door to offer to carry the tray but she was already coming through with it. To say the air was a little tense would be an understatement and he knew it was getting to him. As soon as they were seated with their drinks and biscuits in place, she gave a small cough as if to attract his attention.

"I think we had better address what happened today and then we know where we are." She didn't look up.

"That is probably a good idea." It seemed a bit tame but he still wasn't sure where this was going.

She took a sip of her drink and put the cup down very precisely.

"We may not have the closest marriage, but we have both been faithful and I will not allow anything to change that."

"I understand, I mean that's right." He stumbled as this was unfamiliar territory.

"Whether you realise it or not, I was fully aware of her presence at church this morning and guessed she would be up to one of her tricks, but it was sooner than I thought and she certainly didn't waste any time."

Alarm bells went off in his head.

"You recognised her?"

"Well, I know that kind of person and that's how they work."

There was silence for a moment then she said "But rest assured I don't think she will bother you any more."

"But Sam….."

"Oh Sam, he'll stick his nose into anything and he just took the opportunity to get close to her, take it from me." She gave a short laugh which came out more of a 'ha'.

"So….we won't be seeing her again?" He ventured.

"Oh, you mark my words. She won't venture in this area, ever."

"Well I'm pleased about that, and thank you for your intervention."

She studied the biscuit in her hand.

"I can't think what you are talking about."

Did he detect a faint knowing smirk on her face? There was more to this woman than he had realised but he knew he would rather be on the right side of her than the wrong.

Sam was in his little cottage also reviewing the events of the day. He was glad he had the chance to have a bit of fun while protecting the vicar but he was also very pleased to be near to such a luscious bit of crumpet as he called anything tasty. If only he could have changed his image without it being obvious, then it wouldn't have been just a look but something a bit more substantial.

Chapter 13

Irene woke up with a start. She was having a nightmare of being chased but at the last minute something grabbed her out of the way and threw her on to the ground. In fact the surface was softer as she was in bed.

"Are you ok Mum?" Russ's voice called.

"Um yes, I think so." Her voice was little more than a whisper and he didn't hear it but knew something was wrong. He tapped on her door.

"Come in."

"What's the matter? Are you ill?"

He could tell by the state of her what had happened.

"I…I…was trying to run but I was lifted up high and was going to be dropped. It was horrible."

"It's alright now Mum. You just had a very bad dream. Look you are safe in your own bed."

He had put the bedside light on and saw the sweat was all over her face. He fetched a towel and gently dried it off. She was shaking. Her guardian quickly portrayed to Russ that something had been trying to dig into her memories and when she wouldn't co-operate they tried to frighten her so badly that she would be looking over her shoulder constantly. Russ was forced to do something against his will to stop any effects and this called for strong measures.

"I want you to lie down for a moment Mum."

"Why?"

"Just trust me. I know a way of getting this to go away."

Before she could ask more he had sent her into a semi conscious state and wiped the so called dream from her memory. Within moments she sat up.

"What are you doing in my room?"

It could have looked funny but this was a serious business.

"Well I don't know what you were dreaming about Mum but you were singing at the top of your voice."

"Me? What was I singing?" She couldn't believe it.

"Well it was a mixture of hymns I think, but I just wanted to check you were ok and as you are, I'm going back to bed. Night." And he was gone.

Back in his room he mulled over the thought that Denzil would have been part of this but he had managed quite well on his own plus the guardian of course. He wondered for a moment how often Denzil had ruled everything without him being able to take charge. For the first time he felt in control and realised he never had been. So what kind of a friendship was that? Shouldn't it be give and take in any relationship? He felt a sense of guilt at having such thoughts but maybe it was time for him to open his spiritual eyes and adapt. His own guardian was in total agreement and probably not feeling quite so redundant now.

Russ lay there churning events around in his subconscious. When he had realised that Denzil was going to dig and dig until he found 'three', his first thought was that he would be tunnel visioned, and only be concerned in learning the true identity, whatever it cost. But the question arose as to what that would entail. He would need help. Of course, that was why he had heard that Denzil had sought out Lisa. At first he didn't take too much notice as she was far too below their levels to be able to find out anything that he couldn't. Then it hit him. Of course she would fail but everyone would be watching and all the time the attention would be on her, not him.

"What is he up to?" His logic was working overtime.

If there was one thing he had learned about Denzil during his association with him, it was his skill at diverting people from knowing what he was really doing. He could appear to be acting way below his status but when all was revealed he had often pulled off the seemingly impossible and had exposed so called good spirits for what they really were. Then something else seemed like a coincidence. He was aware of Denzil's progress and the fact that Lisa had a twin. This rang a bell. He had described their own friendship as being twins. And the coincidence with Leon disappearing as had their number three which came back to the quest for three.

The annoying part was that it all seemed to be forming a pattern but there were so many gaps and it had be extremely important or why would Denzil risk his final recall because he would never get another chance. There had to be an element or elements that hadn't yet become obvious and it could involve more souls. That could really stir the pot. Some could be crapping themselves or the equivalent in the spirit world. Maybe it wasn't just a personal vendetta which he had led everyone to believe.

Then another thought hit him and he knew he should have seen through it before. If this, whatever it is, is of a highly dangerous nature, and Denzil didn't want him in the firing line, that was why he made waves and left. Russ could have physically kicked him self for not realising but his friend had been so convincing which brought him back to the fact of how skilfully he operated.

"Well, if you can fool me, what chance have they got?" He mused wondering who 'they' were.

It was now the early hours of Monday and he lay back thinking of how things can change so quickly, and also what the coming week would reveal.

There were still continual discussions going on at the top spiritual levels, and although the very experienced were studying Denzil's actions and hoping he would soon reveal his true purpose, there were those who were really piling on the pressure to 'bring him in' as they put it and inform him that he had lost his right to total recall. It was even suggested that he was working for the other side but that was soon squashed and the order given to never raise it again.

It was becoming very obvious that there were some who were so on edge they must have something to hide, and Denzil was a threat to them. Secretly the highest spirits were enjoying it and felt it should be a lesson to others not to dabble in the wrong brook. The odd indiscretion will always be there, as we know.

Lisa wasn't having much luck and knew the time would run out before she found this person he wanted in one of Russ's lives. After all she didn't know who it would be. She would provide the information and he would pick out who he wanted. She would have to bluff her way through it. Then she had an idea.

"What if it's not a person? It could be a time or a place or a thing, even a pet."

She was very distrusting and wondered if this spirit was simply playing with her and had set her an impossible task. But apart from making her look a fool and having his own kind of fun, what would be the point? There was the possibility of getting a bit of help but she liked to work alone and take the full credit. She couldn't remember if he said it was top secret, but it didn't matter as she kept stuff to herself anyway. But if it was that secret, she could bargain for more reward. As she had come up with so little and this was a laborious task with such a tight time limit anyway, it was making her despondent. She wanted something with a bit more kick to it but she might as well see if anything came up and plod on for now.

Something made her want to know more about her twin, Leon. The memory was so vague and when she had ever tried to find out anything, the shutters came down as though she must never know. But it was always worth another go. She regressed but something was strange. This time there was no block, the area was completely empty and wherever she tried to move she was still in endless space. Suddenly she was wrenched back with such force, not pushed, pulled, so something had dragged her back.

"You stupid little fool. If you hadn't been rescued, you would have gone the same way, into endless obscurity as though you had never been."

"Who is this?" She demanded.

There was no reply.

This was very unnerving and had really unhinged Lisa who thought she could cope with anything. All of a sudden, she felt a bit relieved to be alright and the job became less important, in fact she would say she didn't want it, or she couldn't find anything, and get the hell out of it. Unfortunately, it hadn't satisfied her curiosity regarding Leon. Where was he? Then something shot across her thinking. Although they were twins, she and her brother were not always in the physical together so why not combine the two things. She would take a closer look at Russ's first earth life, not just a quick glance this time.

She traced back to his conception and found to her amazement that he was one of triplets, the other two being female. Although he and one of them were on their first earth life, the other was on a return. But things were not good in the womb. One of the females was evil of the strongest kind and had entered the foetus before the proper spirit could take residence. Immediately she knew who it was for twins have an instinct and she was looking at Lena who was in fact Leon. Russ was the male but she couldn't place the other female. She moved forward in time to the birth, and the good angels had no option but to overcome the evil and destroy it. For the safety of the two good spirits, they were all born but the girl Lena did not survive, leaving Russ and the other female who was on a repeat visit, as twins.

This is what the good angels had carefully guarded from Denzil but the strong evil forces were determined that Lisa should find out and had taken this opportunity to put it to their advantage. Now they could use her as an even stronger tool to finish to the job. It would take two stages. The first to obliterate the male child, Russ, and then destroy the repeat female, Denzil.

To say nerves were twitching, would be an understatement. If there were toilets in the spirit world they would be in continual use. When spirits reach high levels, they haven't always been in that position but have lived many lives and learned everything possible about the ways of good and evil. Many angels had been targeted during their existence but with careful planning, the bad had usually been overcome. Unfortunately, they are just as clever and growing in power in many areas although the ones suffering don't realise what they are up against. It is classed as a high achievement to take down the good forces so the objective is always not to let them get a hold in the first place. This can span centuries, for what is time?

This explains why the good angels can have memories of being used at some point and can't rid themselves of the shame. Being penitent isn't enough because what has happened cannot be undone. But they can partly make amends by assisting in current situations and Denzil was the perfect subject.

They were well aware of his contact with Lisa and some wondered just what his little game could be. He was high enough to have found all this information for himself, so why get her to expose things unnecessarily? It had to be a diversion, which meant he was drawing attention away from the true facts. If it had been any other spirit, they would have been made to stop right there and call a halt, but they knew that if he was on to something which could be big, he must be left to his own devices. They just wished it would be soon and there were still things they hoped he would not uncover for there will always be facts that are best left where they have been hidden.

As the light of Monday spread across the land, all seemed very peaceful to the human eye, and even the spirit world was calm but it wasn't a peaceful stillness. Something was building and there was an air of uncertainty in several areas.

The vicar turned and looked as his wife. She didn't speak but got up, put on her dressing gown and went downstairs to make some tea. He got out of bed and fell to his knees, his arms resting on the bed, eyes closed and his hands together in prayer. The tears were creeping through his fingers as he prayed to all that was holy to help fight the oncoming battle. He knew it wouldn't be easy, but the evil must be outwitted and he had been put in a position to play a key part in its demise. His wife returned and quietly put the tea on the side table then stood behind him and placed her hands on his shoulders. There may only have been two of them in the room but the third power had joined them and together their trio was complete. They joined strength and after protecting themselves, built up such a force, they were ready to play their part in obliterating the opposition.

Russ had decided to go to work, not only because he felt a bit better but he couldn't stand a whole day with his mother fussing round and talking about Lily, God rest her soul, at every opportune moment. He thought she had exhausted the subject but at every chance, up it came again.

"It will be a good job when she finds something else to go on about." He thought, but knew that until after the funeral there was no chance. He had to keep Denzil out of his mind, he was well aware of that, and Vinn wasn't bad company and quite astute so life wouldn't be boring.

"I shall miss going to see Lily."

Russ was on his way out and was tempted to carry on without answering, but he knew that if he did, he'd only get an earful when he got home so better to reply now.

"Of course you will Mum. Why not nip down the local shops? It's in walking distance and you never know who you might bump into. Must dash. Bye."

She stood for a moment. It wouldn't be the same but perhaps it was better than nothing. The only trouble was that people didn't seem to have the time to stop and chat these days, in fact some seem to leave the minute she appeared. Now why would they do that? Then she had another thought. She'd ring Vi. Not the best solution but it was better than nothing and you never knew if she might have something to chew over. She decided to clear away the breakfast things, wash up and then sit down and have a chat.

Denzil had a few more checks to make. He needed to be certain of all facts before he made a move and there must be no untied ends. Everything had to be flawless for it to work. It had been a testing task but he was just about ready to bring it altogether, and then he could close the book, at least for now, for as we know there is no end. Even his plans would be recorded somewhere. The timing had to be perfect, for the total recall slot was almost over but he couldn't do this a minute before or a minute after. There was only one space/time option.

Vinn had always been a little suspicious and realised that Russ wasn't as low a level as he liked anyone to believe but he was wise enough to squash the idea and keep everything as it must appear for now. Guardians are high spirits themselves so to be covering someone higher was usually classed as an honour, but as the reasons could be so delicate, or dangerous, you didn't give any indication of anything other than doing your job. They could mask and cloak anything and give the appearance of what they wanted any watchers to see, so it would be assumed that the subject was only the same level as the guardian.

Lisa had mixed feelings. She couldn't wait to gain a high level status but was a tiny bit apprehensive that Denzil would accept her findings. When he didn't make contact first thing on Monday, the thought hit her that he had considered she hadn't produced the information in time. In her view she had, but she didn't trust him and sensed he would move the goal posts at the last minute. Then another feeling crept over her. There was something very strange about him and it didn't sit well. She was now getting the instinct that he wasn't the good spirit she had believed, and, realising how bad she was, he was using her for his own dirty work. In fact, there had been several instances when he wasn't behaving like a good force, but was this bad? If he was going to elevate her, it would have to be on an evil level because he wouldn't raise her to a good one for obvious reasons.

Now her game could change and it put a totally different light on things. She was playing in her own comfort zone, so bring it on.

Violet was just going to call Janet when the phone rang.

"Hello."

"Hello Vi, I just thought I'd see how you are." It was her sister in law.

"Oh no." Violet thought. "She's going to pester me now her friend has died." But was forced to reply "Hello, how are you doing?"

As soon as the words left her mouth she could have bitten off her tongue because she'd opened the door for a long tirade of self pity.

"Well since you ask, I'm bearing up under the circumstances. But it isn't easy you know."

Violet was able to cut in the pause her sister in law had made for effect.

"I think we both know that Irene, we lost our husbands. And you do have Russell for company."

Irene hadn't expected that and tried to pull back to the matter in hand.

"I'm waiting to hear about the arrangements. You know what I mean."

"Yes I do understand what you're saying." Vi's eyes shot heavenward along with the supressed sigh.

"You must come over sometime. Haven't had a chat for ages."

"Well we do talk on the phone."

"Yes but it isn't the same is it? And there's nothing going on round here worth mentioning, except Lily of course."

Violet had had enough and wasn't in the best of moods for some reason.

"What you're trying to say Irene is that you've got nobody to get any gossip from. Well I haven't got any, so we don't have that much to talk about do we?"

There was a long silence.

"Are you still there?" Vi hoped she wasn't but the line was open.

"I'm here. And may I say, if that's how you feel, don't bother. But you know, you remember who was there for you when you needed them, and who wasn't."

She shouted the last three words and the call was ended.

"Ooooh." Vi mocked. "I bet that went down with a bang." And she wasn't just referring to the handset.

The phone rang again. Surely it couldn't be her. Gingerly she picked it up and said "Hello?"

"Hi Vi. How's your bulges? Ha Ha."

"Oh Janet, thank goodness it's you."

"Well it's nice to be wanted I always say. Something up?"

"No, I've had Irene on again. Wants us to talk more often."

Janet's reply came over as rather a wet raspberry followed by "How lovely for you."

"Shut up you monster. I'm not getting landed with her I can tell you."

"What did you say?" Janet hoped it would be apt.

"Just told her straight, I haven't got any gossip."

"Bet you wish you had though eh?" She giggled.

Vi felt much better now. Janet always cheered her up and before she had chance to say any more Vi cut in with "And before you say it, not swinging on any bell ends."

Janet exploded.

"Listen to yourself woman!" She was nearly crying.

"What, what you on about?" Vi had to laugh although she hadn't a clue why.

"I think you mean bell ropes."

"Isn't that what I said?"

"No!"

As the laughter died down a bit Janet said, through splutters "I will explain next time I see you ok?"

"Well, alright, but why not tell me now."

"Look, just don't say it to the vicar." And she went of on another bout of laughter.

One thing had come out of this happy moment, she didn't give toss for Irene, or her problems. They had a job in hand this morning and so they made arrangements as to what time to meet. Attached to the church was a small hall along with the usual small kitchen and it was their turn to give it a good clean. Janet would be sure to find something hilarious about most of it so it wouldn't be a chore.

"As long as his bell………" She started but Vi cut her off.

Sam was a bit earlier than usual at the vicarage this morning but nobody commented for one good reason. They were expecting him. Although no arrangements had been made verbally, it was as though spirits were getting into position for some reason. He knew the ladies were coming to clean and opened to door to the hall. In the kitchen he switched on the hot water so it would be ready for them. Suddenly he stopped as an icy feeling ran down his back. He couldn't move as though he had been paralysed, his breath was getting laboured and his spirit called out to the vicar for help.

"Let him go." It was a command that echoed through the whole building.

As he was released, he fell over the working surface but hands were there to catch him. Both the vicar and his wife had worked together and ousted the evil from the place. After a moment Sam seemed to have recovered and most people would have told him to go home but this was different. They all had to be together for strength and power and this may have only been the first of many attacks today against anything good. Sam, in body may have appeared old and weak, but in spirit he was a strong force so it must have been something very big that could immobilise him. It also proved to the evil, the power of the other two, for them to be able to expel it so quickly, but this could also make them a target for even stronger evil.

As Violet and Janet reached the hall, the vicar's wife came to meet them. Although she never held anyone in conversation, for some reason it didn't strike them as strange that she should be speaking to them now.

"We need to stay in groups today." She said. "Sam has been, well not too good this morning so we must keep an eye on him."

Although they could never explain it, a bond had been formed between them. They set about getting the cleaning materials together in the kitchen and shortly the vicar joined them.

"Would one of you good ladies mind just helping Sam please?"

"I will."

Janet was there in a minute and followed the vicar into the hall. Although the job was small, another bond had been formed. This continued with nobody being left on their own at any time. It was like an unspoken code and not one person queried the reason, it was something they had to do. They even followed one another to the toilet and although it could have appeared amusing to the onlooker, it was building a defence. Of course, the vicar, his wife and Sam knew they had to protect against something imminent but the other two ladies wouldn't, so the spirits used a method similar to hypnosis. The subjects would do as they were bid without question, and hopefully it would keep them safe under a stronger umbrella of power.

Lisa wanted to do a final bit of poking around on the physical because you never knew what people were hiding in their past and there may just be a little clue which could prove useful. She tried to approach Irene but couldn't penetrate an invisible shield, so her attention turned to Violet but the same thing happened. She was about to leave when she looked again at Janet.

"Best not leave any stone unturned." She thought.

As she approached, Janet was laughing at something as usual with the vicar and Sam. Then they suddenly turned to face Lisa, and a terrific gust of power was aimed at her shooting her backwards.

As she was flung far away, she could hear sadistic mocking laughter and it wouldn't leave her.

"Had enough yet?" The voice was close now.

It took a moment for her to gather her wits but she soon realised who had been playing with her, goading her and sending her on useless quests. This also meant she would not be lifted to a higher level so made the whole thing completely pointless and this stirred up her anger.

"So tell me, do you do this just for amusement? Have you now scored enough brownie points for your recall?"

There was silence.

"Well Mr know-it-all, I have learned a lot about myself. I am not one, I am three people and that's what gives me my strength, and you can stuff your levels, because I will find my own."

Again silence.

"I know you are there, I can feel you."

After a moment the question came.

"You did find what you were looking for, am I right?"

"Why ask? You already know."

There was another long pause before the next insult was delivered.

"You had everything in front of you but you are so slow on the uptake. You still haven't realised."

"What? What haven't I realised?"

"The answer to everything. Three."

Chapter 14

Denzil had moved Lisa to a place that was quiet and they seemed to be looking down on the town although it was hazy.

"Why can't I see it clearly?" She wanted to know and should have expected the answer.

"You have never seen anything clearly. You get by simply from picking up on other people's information. You've never had to sort anything out for yourself, and then when you are given the chance to prove yourself, you cock it up."

"Well….." before she could reply he made it clear that if she wanted to know anything she had better shut up and listen for once. Spiritually or otherwise.

Reluctantly she murmured "I'm listening. Get on with it then."

He paused to let her thoughts settle.

"Lisa, Leon, Lena, which ever you choose to be, are not clever, you will never reach the high ranks and basically are a waste of space."

He intended to go in full blast for she wouldn't like the truth.

"But there is one thing that you are. Evil. Many people think the most evil powers only operate on high levels, but usually they are of your standing, mixing with everything and everyone spreading their viruses often undetected because nobody is noticing them."

He let that sink in but she was portraying a feeling of disinterest.

"You have been used to go round making waves and throwing the scent off the real perpetrators. You do all the simple jobs which people think are unimportant and that is because you are not capable, and never will be of doing the big stuff."

She broke her silence.

"I think you have forgotten. I work alone. I take jobs not orders."

"Oh dear. You just don't get it. They use you."

"No, you are the one who doesn't understand so there's no point in discussing it."

"You killed Lily."

He timed it to perfection. The air was still before she came back at him.

"You can't prove it."

"All right. The evil was placed in Lily."

"But I didn't put it there." She threw back at him.

"No Lisa. Leon did."

This had an immediate effect.

"That is a load of balls. How could I when I was visiting her in the flesh? I can't split into two you know, or three."

"No, but you can flit between any of them changing your image. That's done to confuse the watchers."

"But why would I have done it?"

"Simple. She recognised you from another life and would have exposed you, so you made her appear as though her mind had gone, but you made one big mistake."

"And I suppose you are going to tell me what it was."

He knew she couldn't wriggle out of this one.

"Her language. Everyone has their own particular words, and Leon used one of his."

The hush said it all and it can only be imagined what was going through her thoughts, but best not repeated.

That had to sink in to prove she was not the top dog here. Then she came back with another question.

"It is you isn't it? I mean you've never said but it had to be,"

"If you mean Denzil, you are correct."

He didn't offer any further conversation knowing she would be eager for the whole works.

"Well? What is the next bit of rubbish you are going to accuse me of."

"You thought you'd done so well digging into Russ's past didn't you?"

"You obviously couldn't or you wouldn't have had me......hang on... you knew what I'd find."

He certainly wasn't going to elaborate and admit some of it was more revealing than he imagined.

"Not a pretty story was it?" The words were little more than a breath.

"It's life, it's what we do. Why do you lot always have to make such an issue out of it? Life isn't pretty mate. Stop being so righteous. You lot have your heads buried in the sand. What you don't know can't hurt you. You make me sick."

"So now the real Lisa is coming out. You saw nothing wrong in trying to destroy the other two triplets in the womb with you. A foetus that full of evil was supposed to have been destroyed. And you will forever be seeking revenge for it because you were overcome. But the evil powers must have intervened to prove they could outwit us. Not for your benefit, but just to show they could do it."

Denzil now knew the truth why the high angels hadn't wanted him to expose this as there would be many red faces at the failure of the task to destroy the evil entity for good.

The hush was extreme. He took a moment before adding "If you would do that at that stage, it proves what you would do through a full earth life."

She didn't reply for a moment but then added "That must have been one hell of a shock for you, knowing I was the third."

He let her think about it now but she had another question.

"In that later life when you fell in love with Leon….."

"I didn't fall in love with him, we had a friendship."

"Oh please. You forget I was on the other end of that."

"Yes, until I realised you were evil. Remember?"

She seemed to be planning something. After a moment her tone changed.

"What you do need to realise is, that if you take me down now, you will go with me. I will see to that."

The innocent fumbling little creature had gone and the real image was being exposed. He had drawn her out at last. As her image grew until she was almost towering above him he played his trump card.

"You haven't been very observant have you?"

She stopped. If nothing else, she had to know if he was bluffing.

"Explain."
He waited a moment before he delivered it.
"Three!"
That did it. She seemed to be in a pause position. He remained motionless, knowing she would demand an explanation.
"We've done that. Triplets."
"Oh no, no. You are way off track, but you are so clever, I'm sure it won't take long for you to sort it out. Of course whether or not you understand it is a totally different matter."
He was piling it on to get her to really explode and he felt she wasn't far off. This bit would have to be played with utmost caution or he could lose it, so said simply "Bye."
"No. You will not go until you have explained."
He had given enough time for everyone to be in position as he daren't check because she would have picked up on it immediately. He floated a bit for effect, knowing it would annoy her, but he held the trump card.
"Well, come on. Get on with it." She was agitated now.
"Right. Three."
"Don't keep repeating that." The air was being disturbed with her angry vibes.
"Just explaining. Don't rush it. I want you to fully understand."
He shouldn't have been enjoying it but there was a satisfaction in dangling her for a bit, however it was time for the final blow.
"Your downfall is your lack of observation my dear." He couldn't have been more patronising if he tried and he knew it didn't go down well and he paused before continuing.
"Look around the area. What do you see?"
"Nothing. Now get on with it or you will be sorry."
"Exactly. You see nothing but it is full. It is full of three. Be aware of the groups."
She turned her attention away from Denzil. To her right, the vicar, his wife and Sam. On her left she could pick out Violet, Janet and the vicar's wife again, but she was in the other group as well. Then she saw Sam, Janet and the vicar and they were moving all the time, sometimes coming close then circling so whichever way she looked there was a group of three but they

were mixing it so much it was hard to keep track of them. After a while there seemed to be no gaps and she was completely encased in the swirling cloud and there was no escape.

Then something else happened. She split into three and Leon and Lena were separate to her. The good powers held them awaiting the next move. All that could be heard was Denzil's voice.

"My job is finished. I have isolated you and you will now be disposed of. You will be taken from here never to return." In seconds they had gone and all that could be heard was 'Three.'

The area had to be cleansed and special spirits were there immediately for that purpose, leaving the members of the groups to disperse and return to their physical forms. They would carry on as though nothing had happened and the world would be none the wiser as to the drama that had taken place but in a very small way would be safer.

There was a goodbye that had to be said and time was running out. Denzil approached Vinn and asked him to give him a few moments. It was about midday and Russ was having his lunch outside enjoying the pleasant sunshine. Suddenly he felt an arm round his shoulder and recognised the touch so didn't turn.

"I had a job to do and I couldn't include you and I had to distance myself, but my feelings never changed."

"I knew that inside." Russ answered in thought. "You will have to go now won't you?" He felt the tears at the back of his eyes.

"We knew that." Denzil was also feeling pain of parting.

"Wherever you will be, wait for me."

"I will."

Today would feel different from now on. Russ knew he wouldn't witness Denzil's departure and in a way it was for the best. Vinn was at his side but it wasn't the same. There would always be a hole.

In certain cases where the recall has been interrupted, the portal is available for a limited time and in Denzil's case it was about to close. As he was lifted back to the high realms under the highest protection, he prepared himself for the biggest transition any spirit could experience. He was greeted by the high angels, some of whom didn't think he could possibly pull off the operation, for not only did it mean he would rid the area of the evil attached to Lisa, but the higher power who was controlling her although none may never learn its true identity. The hierarchy had left several false trails through their thought patterns which had hindered anyone tracking him. But now it was time with only earth seconds to go.

One moment he was in the midst of them, the next he had gone.

Total Recall, is difficult to describe accurately as of course no one comes back to tell and any insight is classed as a privilege to only a few. It can happen to the good souls who have achieved outstanding spiritual levels, but it can also be applied to the evil who must be banished forever.

Denzil knew that when he had been selected, there was no turning back and it took a while to understand just what it meant. For anyone to cut off every tie and go to exist in another dimension is daunting, even those in high places.

How the evil are disposed of is not known and should not even be the subject for discussion.

Denzil was in a strange place, he was alone yet not alone, he could see but not in the physical sense, for he was observing solely in a new existence. There was nothing that resembled a body, no angel wings, haloes or beams of light, but something was guiding him for a moment and he felt in communication with someone. He tried to get his bearings but the earth, and the whole solar system had gone. It was part of space, obviously in the universe but there was no sense of direction. Strangely enough he felt a presence was there and he tried to communicate. The answers came to him but from where?

"You have to break all ties and thoughts of where you have been because you don't exist there now and you will never return. The area you know is far away and you will travel to new places with new experiences, and do important work but in a different form."

This was the first time he realised he had no shape, but there seemed to be something remaining. Then whatever it was, evaporated completely and it was just space.

For obvious reasons, it is impossible to explain further.

Russ couldn't concentrate on his work and just wanted to get home. He knew he would never been in contact with Denzil again and it would take a lot of adjusting. He walked into the house and called that he was home but there was no response. There was an eerie emptiness about it and in his present state he found it very unnerving. Where was his Mum? Everything was too quiet. Then he realised that the whole atmosphere had changed, in some ways it was lighter and there was no tension. He dropped his bag on the chair and went all over the house calling her.

She lay on the bed motionless where she had been since Lisa had been terminated. He couldn't bear to look at her face as it didn't look like her and yet he knew it must be. Something seemed to be telling him that everything would be alright now. There was no spirit presence with the body, all that was left was an empty shell that had served its purpose.

Russ knelt and sobbed, not out of sorrow for her but knowing how much his 'twin' had been protecting him knowing he was in the firing line and could have been in danger at any time of his life.

He was also aware he had been right in the middle of both aspects of Total Recall.

THIS IS STRANGER THAN STRANGE MAKE OF IT AS YOU WILL

After the author had finished the novel, she saw this
about the magnificence of 3 6 and 9
by Nikola Tesla
July 10 1856 – January 7th 1943

```
111  222  333
 3    6    9
444  555  666
 12   15   18
 3    6    9
777  888  999
 21   24   27
 3    6    9
```

"IF YOU ONLY KNEW THE MAGNIFICENCE OF
THE 3, 6, AND 9, THEN YOU WOULD HAVE
THE KEY TO THE UNIVERSE"
Nikola Tesla

Information kindly supplied by
MIRACLES FROM YOUNIVERSE

About the Author

Tabbie Browne grew up in the Cotswolds in central England which is where she gets the inspiration for her novels. Her father had very strong spiritual beliefs and she feels he guides her but always with a warning to stay in control of your own mind.

Her earliest recollection of writing was at primary school and it has seemed to play a part at significant times during her life. She thinks it is only when we are forced to take step back and unclutter our minds for a while we realise our potential. This point was proved when she slipped a disc, and being very immobile had to write in pencil as the ink would not flow upwards! At this time she wrote many comical poems which, when able again, performed to many audiences. Comedy is very difficult but you know if you are a success with a live audience.

In 1991 as a collector of novelty salt and pepper shakers, she realised there was no book in the UK devoted entirely to the subject. So she wrote one. Which meant she achieved the fact that it was the first of its kind in the country and it sold well to like collectors not only in the UK but in the USA.

Another large upheaval came when she was diagnosed with breast cancer, and due to the extreme energy draining, found it difficult to work for an employer. So she took a freelance journalist course and was pleased to have articles accepted, her main joy being the piece about her father and his life in the village. Again the inspiration area.

But the novels were eating away inside and drawing on her experience at stamp and coin fairs she wrote *'A Fair Collection'* which she serialised in the magazine 'Squirrels' for people who hoard things.

When she wrote *'White Noise Is Heavenly Blue'* and its sequel *'The Spiral'* she sat at the keyboard and the titles just came to her, as did the content of the books. There is no way she could write the plot first as she never knew what was coming next, almost as if somebody was dictating, and for that reason she could never change anything.

Loves:
Animals,
Also performing in live theatre and working as a tv supporting artiste.

Hates:
Bad manners,
Insincere people.

Printed in Poland
by Amazon Fulfillment
Poland Sp. z o.o., Wrocław